JESUS and JESUSA

Maria Maddalena

BonPasse Exoneration Services. (a Maine non-profit corporation)
P.O. Box 390
Newcastle, ME 04553 USA
001-207-586-6078
Morrison Bonpasse, Executive Director
morrison@bonpasseexonerationservices.org
www.bonpasseexonerationservices.org

Jesus and Jesusa
by Maria Maddalena (pseudonym)

ISBN-10 0983798567
ISBN-13 978-0983798569

TABLE OF CONTENTS

How the world changed – See 2093 Ph.D. Thesis of
Charlotte Amalie Perkins, The Global Social and
Political Impact of the Utopian Novella *Jesus and
Jesusa* as summarized in Appendix B of upcoming
book, *2121*, by Morrison Bonpasse

Foreword

The forward looking novella, *Jesus and Jesusa,* is published in 2014 as the first of a two-book combination with the novel, *2121,* to be published later in 2014, although ostensibly written in 2121. They are both utopian, with *2121* incorporating by "looking backward" the publication of *Jesus and Jesusa* into its story. Each can be read separately, but it's recommended that they both be read, and in order of their publication.

Both books present what may be called realistic utopias, as the societies they describe are believed by the author to be realistic, given what we know about science and human relations. They are optimistic in the sense that present a view of humanity as solving its problems of global warming, overpopulation and wrongful convictions, and emerging in the early 22nd century as a kinder, gentler and smarter species.

The alternatives, which usually seem more likely, are a diminished Earth and a diminished human population unworthy of its good fortune to have evolved this far.

List of Characters
(Dates are dates of birth unless followed by a hyphen and a date of death)

<u>Primary Characters</u>
Jesus, born as Jesus Prescelto, 2014-2089
Jesusa, born as Jesusa Prescelto, 2014-2089
Prescelto, Giuseppe, born as Giuseppe Altacelto –
  Father of Jesus and Jesusa 1979-2076
Prescelto, Maria, born as Maria Prescudo – Mother of
  Jesus and Jesusa 1978-2078

<u>Other characters</u>
Bakhita, Susanna - Pope
Benedict, Arnold – friend and roommate of Patrick
  O'Laughlin
Bush, John Ellis ("JEB") – 45th President of the United
  States. 1953
Donato, Guglielmo Donato - Cardinal in Vaticano.
Eggerickx, Sonja - leader of the International
  Humanist and Ethical Union (IHEU)
Francesco I, Pope 1936
Francesco II, Pope
Friday, Josephine – Dallas Police Dept. Lieutenant
Galvani, Allessandro – Scientist at Universita del Sigli
  di Salerno.
Lawrence, Budge – President Bush's liaison to the GTO
  (Great Transformation Org.).
More, Thomasina – Archbishop of Canterbury.
Obama, Malia – Sec'y General of the United Nations.
Obama, Natasha (Sasha) – Governor of the
  Commonwealth of Virginia.

O'Laughlin, Patrick – Convicted of attempted assassination of Co-Popes.

Pappalardo, Angelo - Scientist at Universita del Sigli di Salerno.

Scheck, Teresa – Attorney and priest.

Sediva, Elvira – Executor of the estate of Alessandro Galvani.

Chronology

2014 Births of Jesus and Jesusa

2020 Nuclear Explosion at Kahuta, Pakistan nuclear facility

2020 "Great Transformation" 50-year campaign begins

2021 Alexandria Treaty between Israel and Muslim/Arab neighbors.

2026 Adoption of a Single Global Currency: mundo.

2032 Graduation from Da Vinci School

2036 March along the Great Wall of China

2037 Graduation from Universitat Heidelberg

2038 Become co-presidents of International Humanist and Ethical Union.

2041 Global Religious Framework.

2042 Vaticano Council IV convenes. Jesus and Jesusa ordained as priests, then cardinals.

2044 Jesus and Jesusa elected Co-Popes.

2045 Temple Mount Accord

2054 Reunification of Roman Catholic and Eastern Orthodox Churches.

2084 Resignations of Co-Popes Jesus and Jesusa.

2089 Deaths of Jesus and Jesusa

Chapter 1 Births of Jesus and Jesusa

On May 30, 2014 twins were born, apparently fraternal boy and girl, to Giuseppe and Maria Prescelto of Paestum,[1] in the province of Salerno, Italia.[2] Giuseppe Altacelto and Maria Prescudo were married on New Year's Day, 2000 at the ages of 21 and 22, respectively. They grew up in neighboring towns, but didn't meet each other until matched by the online dating service, www.italianoamore.com.[3] To make a new start and escape the sexist naming customs, they melded their surnames to become Prescelto. Giuseppe was a mason and stone cutter with his primary work at the Magna Graecia site in Paestum, with its three magnificent temples. He recreated pieces of each temple as they would have appeared at their time of original construction between 600 and 400 B.C. The pieces were then exhibited in the Paestum Archeological Museum, alongside surviving real pieces, or re-cast lookalikes. Sometimes, the pieces were painted as they originally appeared.

Maria was an attorney, specializing in building and real estate law. Growing up, she barely knew of the Paestum temples and only visited them once, when out-of-town relatives came to visit.

Maria and Giuseppe became aware of their infertility around 2003 when they stopped using

1. This is the current Italian and historic Roman name for the site. The Greek name was Poseidonia.
2. Italy. Since 2014, many new words have been introduced into English primarily because of the decision of the Global English Standards Organization (GESO) in 2025 to use the native, local or real spellings of names of people and places. The practice is called RealName. GESO was established by the United Nations in 2018. If the native language didn't use the Latin alphabet, then the best transliteration was used, rather than a translation. This RealName usage is intended to respect the integrity of the named people and places.
3. As of 2014, not a real website.

contraceptives with the intent of raising one or two children, preferably twins. Maria did not look forward to pregnancy, and a single pregnancy was preferable to two. After other methods of overcoming infertility did not work, including medicines and sexual exercises, Giuseppe and Maria were referred to Dr. Pappalardo's Infertility Team at the medical school of the Universita del Sigli di Salerno. This school had a distinguished history as the site of Europe's first medical school, Schola Medica Salernitana, which was most prominent from the 11th through the 13th centuries. One of its most famous graduates and teacher was a woman, Trotula, who wrote medical texts on women's medicine.

Dr. Pappalardo told Guiseppe and Maria that their infertility was unusual in that it had a double cause: his low sperm count and the production by her ovaries of eggs which had an immunal rejection response to his sperm. Still, Maria's uterus seemed healthy, and Dr. Pappalardo heard Maria's request for twins, so the doctor recommended that two fertilized eggs from the same donors be implanted artificially. Two were becoming available in late August, which timing was in synch with Maria's menstrual cycle. The Presceltos were told that the male and female donors were graduate students at the Universita del Sigli di Salerno. For reasons Dr. Pappalardo didn't explain, he didn't want to freeze the eggs once they became available.

Giuseppe and Maria agreed to raise the two children until adulthood, and agreed not to seek the identities of the biological parents, according to standard practices of in-vitro fertilization. The implantation of the two embryos was successful, and Maria's pregnancy was easy and she was happy. As was the normal practice for expecting parents, Maria underwent pre-natal genetic testing, and the fetuses were entirely normal.

After the birth of apparently fraternal twins, they were baptized in the neighborhood parish church. Without prompting from the scientific team, Giuseppe and Maria named them Jesus and Jesusa (Jay-sooz' a). They chose the English spelling for Jesus because Maria had become fluent in English during her one year in a high school in the United States through the American Field Service (AFS). The Espanol spelling was chosen for Jesusa, because it was the most common in their Google search for feminine equivalents for Jesus. Relatives and friends saw the children and called them "angelic," and "divine," but because such terms were commonly used to flatter the parents of attractive children, no further weight was given to such labels.

The friends and relatives were closer to the truth than they realized.

Chapter 2 Foreskin of Calcata – from Roma to Calcata to Roma

The story of Jesus and Jesusa began in Calcata, a small town north of Roma, Italia, and 230 kilometers northwest of Salerno. In January 1983, the town's sacred relic, the foreskin of Jesus of Nazareth, also called the "Holy Prepuce," was removed by an unknown person from a box under the bed of the village priest in Calcata, Don Dario Magnoni. Actually, it was in Calcata Nuova (new) because Calcata Vecchia (old) had been abandoned by most residents in the 1930s after the Government condemned the town due to risks of landslides of volcanic soil, especially during earthquakes. Nearly the entire population of about 400 people moved up the hill to the newly built replacement town. After the feared slides did not occur, some residents returned to Calcata Vecchia and others were attracted by the opportunities for rent-free squatting in abandoned homes. Most of those latter residents later purchased their squatter homes.

The foreskin had remained in the old church, which was named for Saints Cornelius and Cyprian. Pope Cornelius and Bishop Cyprian worked together for the Christian faithful in the third century. Cyprian was martyred by beheading in 258 A.D. Sometime before leaving for a church-related trip to Roma, Don Dario brought the relic from the old church to his bedroom in Calcata Nuova. When he returned from Roma the next week, he found his house had been burglarized. No money was taken, but the "Holy Prepuce" was gone.

As the body of Jesus of Nazareth had ascended, by Christian belief, into heaven, the foreskin from his Jewish circumcision was purportedly one of only two remnants of his body remaining on earth. The other is a section of his umbilical cord which is a relic at the Papal Archbasilica of St. John Lateran in Roma, said to be the most important church of the Roman Catholic faith. It even outranks St. Peter's Basilica at the Vaticano. Of the two bodily relics, and several churches claimed to have a piece of the Holy Prepuce, the foreskin was the more famous or exotic, perhaps because of its sexual location.

While there were only a few relics of Jesus himself, there were hundreds of relics of the Apostles and other saints on display in Western Europa churches. There are skulls, arms, legs, livers, and other parts of most Christian saints everywhere. For many churches, these items were treasured links to the holy past, and the sources of miracles and, not incidentally, monetary contributions to the church.

There were about 30 churches which claimed to have one of the two or three nails which were used to fasten Jesus of Nazareth to his wooden execution cross, and many others which claimed to have a piece of the cross itself. The most famous relic of Jesus of Nazareth, and the one subjected to the most serious testing, is probably the Shroud of Turino which purportedly covered the body of Jesus of Nazareth after his crucifixion.

The Calcata foreskin relic had been in the town since 1527 when a Deutsch[1] soldier was captured in the town with the relic in his possession. He had participated in the "Sack of Roma," and was returning north to Deutschland when captured. He hid the relic in his cell and left it behind upon his release, perhaps fearing punishment if it became known he had taken it from Roma. The foreskin was rediscovered in the jail 30 years later in 1557. It was thereafter displayed in the church in Calcata, and Christian pilgrims were rewarded with indulgences for visiting the site. An indulgence was thought to assist Christians to reduce the spiritual punishment for their forgiven sins.

1. German

Before the Martin Luther-led Protestant divorce from the Church, indulgences were widely sold to raise funds.

The Calcata relic was one of several foreskins in Europe claimed to have belonged to Jesus of Nazareth. In the 12th century, the Abbot of Charroux Abbey in western France asked Pope Innocentius III to decree that the abbey's "Holy Prepuce" was the genuine article. The pope declined to decide and the relic disappeared. In 1856, a workman at the ruins of the Charroux Abbey claimed to have re-discovered the "Holy Prepuce" which had been hidden in the ruined abbey's walls. The owners of the relics in Calcata and Charroux, and other places, argued for the bragging rights for the authenticity of their relics.

The Church found the issue sufficiently embarrassing and distasteful that in 1900, an order was issued that any Catholic speaking or writing about the "Holy Prepuce" would be excommunicated. That order didn't stop the controversies and curiosity, so in 1954 the punishment was increased to the higher level of excommination and shunning. One reason for the continued interest was that January 1 was still celebrated by Catholics as the "Holy Day of Circumcision." To reduce that attention, the Vaticano Council II, 1962-65, changed the name of the holiday to "Octave of the Nativity."

Still, the issue of a foreskin relic continued to surface from time to time among theologians until the relic disappeared from Calcata in 1983. Interest in the foreskin was rekindled by the 2009 publication of the book, *An Irreverent Curiosity*, by David Farley of the United States.

Chapter 3 Cloning the Foreskin

In the 1950's James Watson and Francis Crick, with the inspiration and initially unrecognized assistance of Rosalind Franklin, presented to the world the structure of DNA, the key to the design and propagation of life. Speculation began in the ensuing decades about how DNA could be used to artificially recreate cells, and then organs and finally people, which was described in several science fiction books. Gradually, reality caught up to those books. A big forward step was the cloning of the Scottish sheep, Dolly, in 1996 from a cell taken from a female sheep's mammary gland.

Pope Ionnes Paullus II[1] was advised in 1982 that scientists could, in the foreseeable future, take the DNA from the only known purported remnants of the body of Jesus, his foreskin or his umbilical cord, and use that DNA to recreate a human being. Pope Ionnes Paullus II saw potential danger to the church, and Christianity, too, that the relic could be stolen by others, so he is thought to have taken the prudent step of having the foreskin relic removed in 1983 from the church in Calcata and brought to the Sacred Archives in the Vaticano for safekeeping. It was a secret operation, and speculation arose later that the local priest and/or others had stolen the relic, but no one in the town knew the real story.

At the Vaticano, controversy swirled about the future of the Catholic Church and what role the Holy Prepuce or Holy Umbilical Cord could play in the Church's revival. The use of the Holy Umbilical Cord was rejected by scientists because its container for

1. Pope John Paul II, (1978-2005). He was the third longest serving pope, after St. Peter (Petrus) (33-67) and Pope Pius IX (1846-1878).

several centuries was made of lead, which was thought to have caused damage to the cells of the Cord.

In November, 2011 Cardinal Guglielmo Donato, the newly appointed President of the Pontifical Commission for Vaticano City State, authorized a Catholic scientist to remove a .5 centimeter square of the foreskin relic and evaluate whether the DNA in that fragment could be used to recreate a human being. The scientist, Angelo Pappalardo, of the Universita degli Studi di Salerno, recruited four others for his team in this project. All were sworn to secrecy.

After six weeks of analysis, the team agreed that it was possible to recreate a human being from the DNA in the Holy Prepuce. However, they also agreed not to tell Cardinal Donato the truth. They were scientists first and Catholics second, and they believed that Pope Benedictus XVI, who succeeded Pope Ionnes Paullus II in 2005, would suppress any report of feasibility that the team might issue. Further, they feared for their own safety if they told the Vaticano the truth. If a Pope could authorize a burglary, who knew what he could authorize.

After the report of "no feasibility" was sent to Cardinal Donato, the team of five was not sure what to do. The team had kept the .5 cm square sample, after telling the Vaticano that it had been consumed in the analysis process. Professor Pappalardo then proposed that as scientists they must pursue what they believed to be possible. He recommended that sufficient DNA be extracted to clone not one but two human beings: with one of each sex. The sexual change could be achieved by taking one of the cloned embryos and switching "off" the Y sex chromosome and doubling the X sex chromosome so as to create a female.

He argued, "In this world of gender equality, it would not be fair to produce just a male child from the Jesus foreskin." Prof. Pappalardo proposed that an infertile and married woman volunteer, who is seeking to have children, be found to bear the two children and raise them to adulthood. The other four scientists appeared to be astonished, but agreed that it was possible and that it would advance the science of reproduction, if not the Catholic religion. One member, Alessandro Galvani, expressed optimism but with doubts about the chances of success. He said "I very much want this to work, but no one has ever successfully cloned cells which are this old."

The five members of the team agreed unanimously to proceed with the project. It was agreed further that members of the team would tell no one else of the source of their human DNA, including the prospective mother and father.

The actual cloning was predicted to take approximately four days, after soaking the foreskin sample in a special solution for a week. After the prospective parents were identified, interviewed and approved for the project, "Cloning Day," was set for August 26, 2013, with implantation scheduled for August 30.

Chapter 4 Childhood and college

As Jesus and Jesusa grew, they were clearly happy children and seemed to enjoy every minute they were awake. They didn't need to be taught to share. Gradually, it became more evident that they were different from other children. They spoke in measured cadences, in order that everyone could understand them. They were extraordinarily polite. They were very interested in their father's work at Paestum, to the point of knowing almost as much as he knew. In their teens, the twins were said to have had "wisdom beyond their years." They had an unusual affection for each other as well. Unlike most twins and siblings they showed no signs of conflict with each other.

The education at their primary school was based on the Reggio Emilia approach which stressed the dignity and integrity of the students, even at that young age. That method arose after World War II through the work of educator Loris Magaluzzi in Reggio Emilia which is 350 kilometers northwest of Roma. He was motivated to educate students who would not so willingly surrender individual freedom to future governments, as he had seen happen in Fascist Italia and Deutschland.

Jesus and Jesusa had no violent conflicts with fellow students at school. Whenever there was a controversy or argument between Jesus or Jesusa and another student, it would be settled with an unusual turning of the other cheek or another signal of peace. The other student would cease arguing in every instance. For example, one student bully, Sylvio, took a book from Jesus, who simply said, "If you want it, it's yours. Learn from it. Then give it to someone else and share what you both learned with me. Go. Take it, now." Sylvio was stunned. He never planned to read the book, as the theft was only a prank. Secretly, he returned the book to Jesus the next day, by placing it into his book bag when Jesus had left it for a few moments. The next time they saw each other, Jesus smiled, and Sylvio looked down at the floor.

On another occasion, while playing football, another player intentionally tripped Jesus who fell forward onto his face. The referee didn't see the violation, but other players and his coach saw it and urged Jesus to file a complaint with the school of the errant player. Jesus declined, saying, "Let it be. That player knows what he did, and his teammates know what he did. Let's play the kind of football we know that we can play. We are better than they are." After the halftime break Jesus's team members felt energized by Jesus's forbearance and they outscored their opponents for the win.

Jesusa had different problems. She was beautiful, but cared little about spending time on her hair or skin or wearing jewelry. Sometimes a jealous girl would mock Jesusa for her appearance and Jesusa might respond, "I am here on this earth to help others and not to enhance my own looks." For a 12-year old, this was extraordinary.

Recognizing that their children were special, Giuseppe and Maria enrolled them in 2028 in the Da Vinci School, a secular humanist private boarding school run by the Italian Secular Humanist Foundation, a member of the Global Secular Humanist Movement. The school was in the former Benedictine Abbey in Santa Maria di Castellabate, about 70 kilometers south of Salerno. They wanted their twins to learn about the world through the lens of every religion and not just one.

The Da Vinci School was founded in 1978 by a disciple of A.S. Neill at Summerhill in the United Kingdom. The emphasis of the school was on student initiative and responsibility, and this program was well-suited to Jesus and Jesusa.

For their senior year project, they chose to study wrongful convictions and the death penalty. Italia has an honorable place in the pantheon of countries leading the world toward the abolition of capital punishment. In 1786, one of Italia's predecessor countries, the Duchy of Toscana[1] with its capital in Firenze,[2] was the first modern state to abolish the death penalty. Subsequent Italian governments, especially the Mussolini Fascists in the years 1922-43, legalized the punishment, but used it infrequently, and it was finally abolished in 1948. The last executions were of three civilian murderers by firing squad in 1945.

In 1994, Italia proposed at the United Nations a worldwide moratorium on the use of capital punishment. The resolution lost by eight votes. In 2007, Italia led the European Union to propose a similar resolution, based in part upon the U.N.'s own 1948 Declaration of Human Rights. It passed by a vote of 104 to 54 with 29 abstentions. Subsequent efforts in 2008 and 2010 were approved with similar votes.

The project for Jesus and Jesusa was on two levels. First, they studied the conviction, and execution by crucifixion, of their namesake, Jesus of Nazareth, for treason against the Roman Empire. It was a wrongful conviction, because he had argued for the separation of church and state, and not the overthrow of the Roman occupation of Israel, when he said, "Render unto Caesar the things that are Caesar's, and unto God the things that are God's."[3] He also said, "My kingdom is not of this world."[4] To the Romans, a man who was said to be the King of the

1. Tuscany.
2. Florence.
3. Book of Matthew, 22:21.
4. Book of John, 18:36

Jews, and who spoke of his "kingdom" was enough of a threat to warrant execution, and crucifixion was the standard method used in the occupied territory of Israel. In other parts of the Empire, even more cruel methods were used, such as being eaten by lions in the Colosseum.

At one point in their research, Jesus mused to Jesusa, "Have you ever wondered what symbol Christianity would now be using if Jesus had been simply imprisoned or executed in some other way, such as stoning or to be killed by animals or gladiators in the Colosseum? Perhaps a statue of a lion?"

Jesusa responded, "You know, men are weird, sometimes. I never would have thought of that question, but come to think of it, it's an interesting idea. Symbols are very important and the more elegant and simple they are, the more powerful and persuasive. Where would Christianity be without the cross?"

The second level of their interest in wrongful convictions began with the case of Derek "Rocco" Barnabei who was executed in the U.S. State of Virginia in 2000 for the 1993 murder of his 17-year old friend and occasional sexual partner, Sarah Wisnosky. Twenty-six at the time of Sarah's death, Barnabei was born in 1967 in the U.S. to Italian parents, hence the interest in Italia in his case. Barnabei was seen with Wisnosky on the night she disappeared, and he had driven the next day to his home in New Jersey. However, that trip was pre-planned, as he had told friends, to help his mother celebrate her birthday. Wisnosky's body was found in the Lafayette River in Norfolk. Derek asked for DNA testing, which was not finally performed until a few days before his execution. It showed his DNA in her body, but that was not a surprise as he had already acknowledged having consensual sex with her the day before her murder. Similarly, his DNA was under one of Wisnosky's fingernails, but not under a fingernail which also had her blood, presumably from the fatal assault. Barnabei passed a polygraph exam which he voluntarily took after his arrest, but the report of that test was lost by the police. While on death row in August, 2000 Barnabei offered to take another polygraph examination, but the State of Virginia did not grant the request. The case for his innocence was strong enough that there was a worldwide campaign to stop his execution so that the investigation of his case could continue. Pope Ionnes Paulus II wrote to Governor Gilmore of Virginia to urge that the execution be stopped. However, on September 14, 2000, Barnabei was killed with a lethal injection. His last words to his family were "I am truly innocent of this crime...Eventually the truth will come out." On his gravestone is the message, "The fight goes on," and his mother continued that effort.[5]

After much study and discussion, Jesus and Jesusa prepared a report and a video about the Barnabei case and wrote to Governor Natasha (Sasha) Obama to ask her to appoint a panel to re-investigate the case. Jesus and Jesus also asked the International Criminal Court to investigate the case for violations of Crimes against Humanity.

"Do you think anyone will care?" asked Jesus of Jesusa.

"Probably not," she replied. "Maybe, maybe not, but it was good to try. The fight goes on."

To their surprise, Governor Obama did appoint a committee of five people, including two lawyers, two private investigators and a DNA expert to investigate the case. After eight months, the Committee unaminously concluded in 2033 that Barnabei was

5. The website about the case is at http://www.barnabei.com. His case is one of 18 described in the book by Richard Stack, *Grave Injustice – Unearthing Wrongful Convictions.*

wrongly convicted and recommended that the Governor posthumously pardon him and pay compensation to his family. This was not a declaration of innocence, but an acknowledgment that the judicial process had failed in the Barnabei case.

A similar conclusion was reached 66 years earlier when Governor Michael Dukakis issued a declaration in 1977 that the Massachusetts justice system had failed Nicola Sacco and Bartolomeo Vanzetti who were executed by electrocution in Massachusetts in 1927 for robbery and murder. Sacco and Vanzetti were both born in Italia and had emigrated to the United States, and their cases had aroused even more international protest than the subsequent Barnabei case.

In June 2032, at the age of 18, Jesus and Jesusa Prescelto graduated from the Da Vinci School. They chose this day to drop their surname and be known only by their first names, or their mononym. In music history, they had learned how the New Jersey singer, Madonna Louise Ciccone, born in 1958, renamed herself "Madonna." Similary, Cher was born as Cherilyn Sarkisian. Jesus and Jesusa felt that perhaps they had a mission on earth and their mononymous names were closer to their destiny. At some level, they knew they were not Presceltos, but Giuseppe and Maria did not take offense at the change because they knew that their children were special.

At school, Jesus and Jesusa wore traditional uniforms, with blue pants and white collared shirts and ties for boys, and blue skirts and blouses and ties for girls. The boys' ties were blue with white prints of Leonardo Da Vinci's "Vitruvian Man," with a naked man inside a square figure and a circle. The girls' neckties had print outlines of the Mona Lisa, as painted by Da Vinci.

In an effort to begin moving the school to less sexist clothes choices, Jesusa asked the Head of School if she could wear pants, with a blouse and the

Mona Lisa tie. At first the school resisted, but the teachers knew how determined Jesusa could be for a cause she felt was just, so she was allowed to wear pants like the boys. Soon, other girls followed suit and they asked for a schoolwide vote on their uniforms. The choice was either to continue the current system or change to pants and a blouse for everyone, together with a new school tie that had both the "Vitruvian Man" and the Mona Lisa images. The school agreed to the vote, but the Head of School said the rules could be changed only by a 75% vote. With the social media buzzing, Jesus and Jesusa were able to secure an 82% vote for the change.

When not in school, the twins saw that they had similar tastes in clothes and that they often fit into the same clothes. Jesusa's body became more feminine, but her breasts were modest and her hips were not much wider than her brother's. Neither liked collars, so they cut them from their shirts, when they couldn't purchase shirts without them. They also removed shirt pockets as Jesusa didn't use them as such use would bring further unwanted attention to her breasts. Since Jesusa couldn't use the shirt pockets, Jesus agreed that it was unfair that he should use such pockets, so they removed them from all their shirts. They both wore pants.

Jesusa said to Jesus, "Why should my clothes show more of my skin than yours? What's up with that? In this day and age, which gender is the initiator of contacts and which is the initiatee?"

The words "initiator" and "initatee" were awkward for her, but they were the only words she could think of that avoided stereotypes. Using "predator" and "prey" made relationships sound barbaric, and "aggressor" and "aggressee" sounded violent. "Aggressee" seemed to be a euphemism for "victim."

When they found that they fit into each other's clothes, they began purchasing two of everything. At

20

first, they wore the same clothes when appearing together at parties, but gradually they were wearing the same clothes most of the time. The practice was noticed and a few photos made it to Facebook where they went viral. Soon, many couples, gay and straight, began dressing in the same style clothes, even if they weren't the same size.

Their intellectual and spiritual passion was to learn more about the religions of the world, in the hope that there was common ground among them. From the Bellagio Center Foundation, they obtained a travel grant for 15 months, until their delayed entry into the multinational campus program at the Universitat Heidelberg in Deutschland. Staying at student hostels, they traveled to Espana, Africa and South Asia where they stopped to work at Mother Teresa's Nirmal Hriday (Home for the Dying) in Kolkata.[6] Jesus and Jesusa had never been close to anyone dying before, and their six months in Kolkata were among the most important of their lives. Dying with dignity was better, they came to see, than a painful struggle to breathe each additional breath.

They had learned English and Arabic at the Da Vinci School and those two languages, together with the Latin-based Italian, allowed them to talk easily with most people they encountered. English was the first or second language of approximately 1.5 billion people. When their learned languages were insufficient, Jesus and Jesusa used their "Lingua Mundas," the near-instantaneous computer translators. The devices were small enough so Jesus and Jesusa usually carried five or six in their purses or bags, in the event that others needed them for a group conversation. In a conversation, a person would

6. Formerly spelled by the British as Calcutta. The city has no connection to the Italian town of Calcata.

hear in his/her earphone the translations of what participants were saying.

Their first year at Heidelberg, beginning in the fall of 2033, was spent at the Deutschland campus, with subsequent years in Johannesburg, Boston, and Beijing. They studied as much science as possible, together with courses about ethics, justice, religion and utopias.

Transportation to these international campuses used to be an ethical and cost problem for colleges, most of which had joined the "Fossil Fuel Divestment" campaign and the "Campaign Against Carbon Capitalism." With every country, there was now enough alternative energy to keep buildings warm or cool, as needed, and power the enormous computer and lighting systems, but fuel for air travel was a problem. Fortunately, environmentally sound jet fuel became available with the development of syn-gas (for synthetic gas) which was derived by a process of recombining carbon dioxide and water, when exposed to metal oxides under intense heat provided by concentrated solar reactors. The syn-gas was then converted into kerosene for aviation and other fuels, such as diesel and gasoline as needed. When those fuels were burned, they created carbon dioxide, but no more than was recombined at the beginning of the process. So the process was CO_2 neutral. Although being CO_2 neutral was not good enough to warrant burning wood and biomass, necessity sometimes overcame environmental preferences, so the syn-gas program was a global exception. The syn-gas process became commercially competitive with fossil fuel sources around 2021. One innovative oil and gas refiner, Earth Fuel, Inc., switched completely to syn-gas and used that switch for its major marketing push.

Among the incentives for the development of syn-gas was the clarification that global carbon taxes, which were generally implemented in the 2020s, were to be applied only to fossil fuel carbon, e.g. coal, oil, natural gas, and not to synthetic carbon-based fuels, and not to wood and other bio-sustainable fuels which were used out of necessity. The goal of the carbon taxes, even if applied after so much carbon had already been pulled from the ground, was to require that the carbon extracting industries pay for the cost of sequestering the carbon from the atmosphere and returning it to underground storage.

Also, the previous tax subsidies, worth approximately 200 billion mundos annually, for fossil fuel development were withdrawn and either devoted to reducing national debts or applied to green energy development.

The newer planes needed less fuel because of the increased efficiency of the solar collectors on their upper surfaces. Using a unique combination of composite graphene and aluminum alloy, the planes' solar collectors were able to collect 20% of the energy they needed for propulsion and internal electrical needs. As planes usually flew above the clouds, and increasingly flew during daytime, this source was more intense and reliable than on the ground.

Another technological boost for movement away from fossil fuels came from the development of solar-powered hydrogen crackers, which led to cheaper availability of hydrogen for hydrofusion plants and, in greater quantity, for fuel cells.

Together with the global boycotting of the stock of fossil fuel companies, the development of syn-gas and cheaper hydrogen cracking ensured the global cessation of further exploration for in-ground fossil fuels. Existing wells continued in operation until exhausted, but the old wells were not updated with new extraction technology and new wells were no longer drilled.

Sometimes, Jesus and Jesusa would share "Eureka!" or "Ah Haaa!" moments which would clarify their understanding of the world, and solar energy was one of them. In an "Energy 101" class at Heidelberg, their professor circulated a list of "Key Points" about solar energy. They recalled two examples and posted them on their shared Facebook page. They also had their own separate Facebook pages.

- More solar energy hits the earth every two hours than all the energy, 750 exajoules,[7] humanity consumed during 2033.
- Those 750 exajoules could be supplied by solar collectors occupying about 600,000 square kilometers[8] of land (i.e. a square 774.6 kilometers on each side, or the distance from Portland, Maine to Baltimore, Maryland).
- More solar energy hits the earth every hour than the energy in all the earth's annual oil and coal production combined in the year 2014.

Making international travel easier was the use of United Nations passports, which were now held by about a billion people. Originally, the UN documents were introduced as a way to raise funds for the organization, but their popularity ballooned when people saw them as a way of declaring their solidarity with other peace-minded people. The message was

7. A joule is the work required to produce one watt of power for one second, or one "watt second," which is 1/3,600 of a kilowatt hour. An exajoule is one quintillion (10^{18}) joules.
8. This land area is slightly larger than the island of Madagasgar with its 587,041 square kilometers, and substantially smaller than Texas and Afghanistan with their 695,662 and 652,230 sq. km, respectively.

that UN passport holders considered themselves
citizens of the Earth first, and citizens of countries
second, and then citizens of states, provinces, cities
and towns.

During the long flight to South Africa, Jesus and
Jesusa watched the classic 2006 documentary film,
"An Inconvenient Truth," by the former U.S. Vice-
President, Al Gore. The movie saddened them because
they hadn't fully understood that many people in the
world already knew in 2006 about the dire fate of the
world. Further, the movie didn't shake the world's
decision makers as it should have, even though Al
Gore won the Nobel Peace Prize in 2007, together with
the United Nations' Intergovernmental Panel on
Climate Change. As Jesus and Jesusa both
understood English well, they chose to listen in
Afrikaans, the official language of South Africa which
they were seeking to learn. Using the subtitle option,
they also saw the words at the bottom of their screens
as they were listening to them. The oral translation
and written subtitle options were added to all new
movies, and retroactively to many, beginning in 2021
in order to increase viewers' understanding. It had
been found that many moviegoers couldn't hear the
words in movies, even when they filmed were in their
own native languages. A typical problem was that of
the U.S. moviegoer who would watch a movie made in
England and not understand most of the dialogue
because of unfamiliar accents and words. The default
subtitle option was the intended language of the film.
As part of the global campaign for literacy and
education, it was important that movies, especially
documentaries, be easily understandable.

At the Johannesburg campus in 2034-35, Jesus
and Jesusa studied two major South African figures
who contributed to the transition to the "Great
Transformation" in human life: Mahatma Gandhi and
Nelson Mandela. Born in India and educated in

England, Gandhi's first work as a lawyer was in South Africa where he developed his ideas about peaceful resistance to unjust laws, and about his vegetarian diet. In South Africa, the people of color were discriminated against, although not to the extent of the subsequent apartheid regime during approximately the years 1948-94. In 1915, at the age of 46, Gandhi returned to India and led efforts for independence for British colonial India, which then included what is now Pakistan and Bangladesh, and for the rights of women and the "untouchables." Importantly, Jesus and Jesusa learned of Gandhi's heartbreak at the religious strife which broke out after independence for India and Pakistan in 1947. People killing each other because of their religions perplexed and frustrated them, and seemed counterintuitive.

"Isn't religion about affirming the best in humanity?" asked Jesusa of Jesus.

Nelson Mandela was born in 1918 to tribal royalty and, like Gandhi, was educated in the law. He was a political activist in the struggle for Black African justice and political representation in South Africa. Influenced by Gandhi's work in South Africa, Mandela's initial work was nonviolent, but as the white minority moved South Africa toward extreme apartheid, and as nonviolence failed to achieve the goals of fair representation for black South Africans, Mandela joined the Communist Party and actively supported acts of sabotage. It was for those acts that he was convicted in 1964 of conspiracy to overthrow the government, and was sentenced to life imprisonment. Almost 20 years of that sentence was served in the notorious Robbens Island prison. His stature, his continued thirst for knowledge, and his ability to communicate with people of all political beliefs led to the increasing recognition of his leadership of the Black African movement. In 1990, he was freed from prison and later became the first elected Black president of the Union of South Africa.

Jesus and Jesusa met with Mandela's family and supporters, which prompted them to discuss their futures. The Mandela children were struggling with their roles which birth thrust upon them.

"What do you think we should do?" asked Jesus to Jesusa, knowing that they had already pledged to each other that they would work together to improve the world in some way.

"We don't know, yet," said Jesusa. "But, we do know that we have been inspired by nonviolence and communication. We'll just have to keep exploring options."

The "Great Transformation" was a global political and social movement which began in 2020 primarily to save the planet Earth from humanity. It was triggered by two disasters of that year. First was the South Pacific typhoon, Chanthu, which caused 45 million deaths and 2.1 trillion U.S. dollars of damage. Next was the nuclear explosion in Kahuta, Pakistan which killed 80,000 people. After those disasters, people around the world said to each other, "Enough is enough." That is, the foibles of mankind were now coming intolerably close to causing the extinction of humanity, and it was time for well-meaning people around the world to work together to transform the future.

With funds contributed from several global foundations and from a global "kickstarter" campaign, a new networked organization, Great Transformation Organization, was created with a website, www.greattransformation.org.[9] It became known as GTO. The organization sought to bring people together to find common ground to solve problems. Among

9. As of 2014, not a real website.

other programs in its 50 year campaign, the GTO promoted solutions to these problems:

- global warming. For too long, said the GTO leaders, governments had ignored the warnings about global warming. It was time to stop global warming by reducing the concentrations of carbon dioxide and methane in the atmosphere to pre-Industrial Revolution levels.
- demilitarization. This campaign combined the reduction of nuclear weapons, pursuant to the Non-Proliferation Treaty, with the efforts within countries, led by Costa Rica, to eliminate military expenditures entirely. These countries had police forces to provide security and suppression of crime, but no need for the expensive toys of the generals and admirals.
- education. In order for the Great Transformation to be successful, the global public needed to be educated. Literacy needed to be brought to 100% and every human needed to understand basic information about science, life and Earth. It was not enough that everyone could read. Reading rational information about the true "facts of life" was critical.
- communication/computers. Every human being with the ability to speak and think needed to be connected to the global electronic/computer network through one or more devices, beginning with a smart phone.
- judicial resolution of international disputes. GTO urged the universal use of the International Court of Justice to resolve disputes among countries, such as territorial disputes.
- civil dispute resolution. At the non-state level, the GTO encouraged the submission of all disputes to civil forums, such as mediation, arbitration, courts, and legislatures. The GTO called for the end of the misclassification of "terrorism" as an

end rather than a means. That is, if people sought to terrorize others for the purpose of causing fear for its own sake, that was to be dealt with as a common crime, and not as an act of war against a country. If people used violence to achieve political ends, such violence had always been classified as criminal. If terror was part of that violence, then the level of the crime and the eligible punishment was increased.

- population stabilization and reduction. The GTO sought the reduction of unexpected and unwanted pregnancies, as part of the effort to stabilize and reduce the size of the human population. Conservatives sought to save money from the anticipated reduction in the need for government services, and liberals sought to enhance the lives of young women.

- reduction of use of incarceration as criminal punishment. Conservatives sought to reduce expenditures that could be better used for reduction of government debt, and to enhance the value of personal liberty; and liberals sought to reduce the unequal treatment of minorities by judicial systems around the world. Legalization of recreational drugs was part of this campaign.

- adoption of a Single Global Currency. The people of the world wanted stable money, and no longer could tolerate the absurdities of the multicurrency system.

- better nutrition for all humanity. This was to be achieved by eating foods lower on the food chain, with less cooking, and by severely reducing the consumption of meat and fish.

- fair and free elections. The GTO sought publicly funded elections around the world, pursuant to its faith that if the people of the world were informed with the truth from unbiased sources, they would vote for what is best for themselves, their families and the Earth. It was no longer tolerable that the results of elections depended upon the bank accounts of those seeking office.

The Great Transformation Organization was the rallying point for people around the world, formerly called the "silent majority," who simply wanted a better world for their children, and were fed up with the old solutions, or with pleas that there were no solutions.

The ideas embraced by the GTO had been proposed by others, but the new organization brought to the table what it called "FORTHINK," which was short for "Forward Thinking." The supporters of GTO were called "forthinkers." The key to this concept was that the future counted as much as the present when considering action and funding. One aspect of forthinking was the consideration and payment of external costs whenever considering actions and funding. For example, GTO forthinkers successfully argued that a builder of a building which was to replace another nearby building had to provide a plan for the demolition or re-use of the former building, rather than leaving the old building to deteriorate and impose visual and other costs upon its neighborhood. The biggest boost for forthinking was the campaign in the early 21st century to legalize recreational drugs. Reform advocates compared the total costs of prohibition, including the forward external costs of incarceration, with the benefits, including taxation, of legalizing drugs. When compared directly, the benefits of legalization outweighed the costs by a ratio of 5:1.

Forthinking encompassed a new, while resurrecting the old, way of looking at debt, which was that it should be avoided, except in unavoidable and unpredictable circumstances. Borrowing for purchases of consumer products and services did not fit either category. In the 21st century, before the universal availability of health insurance or coverage, the best justification for personal borrowing was the payment of unanticipated health costs. That justification no longer existed after the adoption of publicly funded universal health care. Similarly, liability and property insurance protected against most other unanticipated costs. On the national scale, money could be borrowed to finance wars, as the U.S. did for during World War II, but during the GTO period, and thereafter, there were no large scale wars.

Until modern times, borrowing was discouraged. The Bible disdained debt and excessive consumption, e.g. "The rich ruleth over the poor, and the borrower [is] servant to the lender."[10]

Shakespeare presented Polonius in Hamlet, who said to his son, Laertes,

"Neither a borrower nor a lender be;
For loan oft loses both itself and friend,
And borrowing dulls the edge of husbandry."[11]

Benjamin Franklin summarized the pre-industrial era view of debt with his saying, "Rather go to bed supperless than rise in debt." The recommended way to finance a purchase or a project was to save for it, instead of paying interest for years afterwards. At 4% interest, a 10,000 mundo loan for a five year term would cost 1,049 mundos, or more than 10% of the original loan amount, in interest.

By the mid-20th century, John Maynard Keynes had persuaded a generation and its successors that it was good policy to borrow money to prime the pump of an economy. However, what people, voters and nations forgot was that the periods of borrowing needed to be balanced with periods of saving. The ease of borrowing by nations was communicated to citizens who overloaded themselves with debt for education, consumer products, and homes.

10. Proverbs 22:7.
11. Act 1, Scene 3.

The tide against debt turned when the adoption of a Single Global Currency, managed by the Global Central Bank within the Global Monetary Union, led to near-zero inflation, which reduced global interest rates. When debtors and citizens realized that they would be paying off debts in the future with money that was maintaining its value rather than being devalued through inflation, the enthusiasm for debt diminished. Forthinkers persuaded the world that such borrowing for the present was not worth the future cost.

Another benefit of the mundo was that the world no longer needed the U.S. to finance the expansion of the global money supply through its own trade and government fiscal deficits. Without that need, purchasers of U.S. debt were less willing to lend money to the U.S. That caused interest rates on government debt to rise, which also led to decreased U.S. borrowing.

During his term, former President John Ellis Bush ("JEB") lauded the creation of the GTO and supported most of its objectives. He said, "We have to learn from our new techniques for educating people about the real world and reversing global warming. He appointed his Phillips Academy classmate and businessman, Budge Lawrence, as special liaison to the GTO.

Another connection to the Great Transformation was President Bush's close relationship with Pope Francesco I[12] who saw the need to change the views of his church and the world toward global warming and

---

12. Known as Pope Francesco, he was not designated as Pope Francesco I until after the election of his successor who chose the name, Francesco II. Both were named after St. Francesco of Assisi, 1182-1226, who was born with the name Giovanni di Pietro di Bernardone. Giovanni's father was on a business trip to France when Giovanni was born, and upon his return, the father called his son, Francesco, which is Italian for the "Frenchman."

non-proliferation. Brought up as an Episcopalian, Bush had converted to Roman Catholicism, the religion of his Mexican-born wife.

During the next few years, and into his second term, Bush helped move the United States toward acceptance of its new role in the world which was as an equal member, albeit large, of United Nations rather than as the world's policeman. Further, he spoke of the U.S.'s large responsibility for global warming because of the disproportionate proportion of U.S. generation of CO_2, as compared to the rest of the world. With only 4% of the world's population, the U.S. was still generating 17% of the world's carbon dioxide, and its historical proportion was even larger. "It is time to reduce the net U.S. share," said Bush, "to less than four percent and then to zero." Subsequent U.S. presidents and governments continued to pursue those goals.

For their next academic year, 2035-36, Jesus and Jesusa went to Boston and Cambridge. They studied at Harvard, the U.S. affiliate of Universitat Heidelberg. While there, they studied the 19th century utopian communities at Fruitlands in Harvard, Mass., and Brook Farm in West Roxbury, Mass. These were communities which arose in response to the unhealthy conditions of the Industrial Revolution in the U.S. They faded away for the same reasons as all the other utopian communities: they asked too much from the people who lived there. It was a mistake to ask people to depart too far from their human nature.

One earlier group, the Shakers, were as much religious as utopian. They were a spinoff group from the Quakers in England and from the beginning they stressed the leadership role of women. One of the first Shaker preachers was Jane Wardley, who was followed by Ann Lee, who claimed to be the Second Coming of Christ, despite the gender difference. Formally called the United Society of Believers in Christ's Second

Appearing, Ann Lee led a group of eight Shakers to the U.S. in 1774. By 1790, the group had established written agreements whereby new members contributed all their property and their future labor to the Society. They also pledged to remain celibate. When married couples joined, their marriages were essentially terminated as they were required to live in separate dormitories. The population of Shakers grew rapidly through recruitment, and many Shaker communities were established in the eastern U.S.

What attracted Jesus and Jesusa to learn more about the Shakers was their belief in the equality of men and women. Their work roles might be different, but their essential equality was respected. Jesus and Jesusa saw that the Shakers spread faster than other sects not by reproducing with children, but by communicating a message of hope and faith. Later, it became clear that there was no Second Coming, and the Industrial Revolution reduced the costs of many products which competed with those manufactured by hand by the Shakers. With less faith, and less prosperity, the Shakers foundered. As the sexual repression of the Victorian era was subsiding in the late 19th century, the celibacy of the Shakers seemed less attractive for future members, just as the Roman Catholic Church's celibacy rules for priests and nuns led to the declines in their numbers until the Vaticano Council III eliminated the celibacy requirement in 2023 and permitted women to become priests, bishops, cardinals and even popes.

Only two hours from Boston was Hartford, Connecticut with one of the homes of Harriet Beecher Stowe, the author of *Uncle Tom's Cabin*. Joined with the home was a museum with a small collection of works by Charlotte Perkins Gilman, who was a grandniece of Stowe, through Charlotte's father Frederic Beecher Perkins. Gilman, who acquired that surname upon marriage, was a feminist writer, speaker and suffragette. She wrote the utopian novel, *Herland*, which first appeared in Gilman's magazine, *Forerunner*, in 1916. It wasn't published as a standalone book until 1979. The book describes a society of women, who have been without men for about 2,000 years and reproduce themselves asexually. They knew nothing of war or violence and certainly suffered no domination by men. Jesusa was especially interested in Gilman's personal independence from convention and the manner of her death. Gilman was diagnosed in 1932 with incurable breast cancer. She publicly advocated euthanasia for the terminally ill, and in 1935 she committed suicide with an overdose of chloroform. Her suicide letter was clear, "When all usefulness is over, when one is assured of an unavoidable and imminent death, it is the simplest of human rights to choose a quick and easy death in place of a slow and horrible one."

Another utopian community which interested Jesus and Jesusa was in New York, but *Walden Two* was fictional and its author, B.F. Skinner was from Harvard and Boston. Skinner died in 1990, but the twins were able to talk with some of his former students who were now professors. They discussed Skinner's 1971 non-fiction book, *Beyond Freedom and Dignity*, which argued for the "cultural engineering" which later became part of the global Great Transformation campaign. The idea was that the study of psychology had become sufficiently advanced, especially operant conditioning, that appropriate positive reinforcements for desired behavior could be established by governments.

The contemporary criticism of *Walden Two* was that the design of the reinforcements seemed to come from one person, the fictional T.E. Frazier, who could be therefore characterized as a dictator. Instead, it was said to be perfectly legitimate for a democratic government to decide what behaviors should be rewarded with positive reinforcement and what behaviors should be discouraged.

The other intellectual focus for their Boston term was the issue of wrongful convictions which they had studied in their senior year at Da Vinci School. Near Boston was Middlesex County where Kenny Waters and Dennis Maher were separately wrongly convicted of murder and rape, respectively, in the 1980's. They were both exonerated through DNA testing after 18 and 19 years in prison. The Waters case became widely known when it was the subject of the 2010 docudrama movie, "Conviction."

Jesus and Jesusa met with the current District Attorney for Middlesex County who proudly told them that there had not been a wrongful conviction in the county since 2021. That conviction, for murder, was vacated six months later after an internal investigation by the County's own Conviction Integrity Unit. It was determined than a technician in the DNA laboratory had a romantic relationship with the investigating police officer which led him to alter the DNA-test results.

Jesus and Jesusa visited prisons in Massachusetts, including the facility at Shirley which was on the site of a former Shaker village. They learned that the DNA revolution had led to a dramatic change in the U.S. justice system by providing irrefutable proof that innocent people were being convicted. In the past, this truth was known by many defense lawyers and some prosecutors, and certainly by those innocent victims of the system who went to prison and were sometimes executed. The DNA revolution forced the truth upon lawyers and people within the justice system and upon the citizens who were served by, and sometimes judged by, that system.

In 2014 a National Commission on Forensic Science was established to extend, as much as possible, to other forensic sciences the precision which had been achieved with DNA. In 2015, the Commission issued a sweeping report which highlighted the deficiencies which had sent thousands of innocent people to prison and allowed others to be "wrongfully free," and therefore free to commit more crimes. New standards were proposed for scientific proof in many areas including: arson, ballistics, fingerprints, lie detector tests, tire tracks and eye witness identifications. The Commission forecast that the adoption of its proposals would reduce the wrongful conviction rate in the U.S. to less than .1%. The Commission compared this goal to the previous estimates of wrongful conviction in the range of 1-5%. The Commission recommended that these standards be implemented as soon as possible, beginning with a five year campaign, and that all the cases of the people who were convicted by use of the earlier, less rigorous, standards be thoroughly re-examined.

A first step was to send to every inmate in the country an invitation to declare his or her innocence on any of several levels:
1. Completely innocent, with no involvement in the crimes for which convicted.
2. Innocent by reason of being a juvenile, under the age of 18, at the time of the offenses.
3. Partially innocent, but convicted and sentenced as if the sole perpetrator.

The plight of the guilty, but grossly and unfairly oversentenced, had to wait for their justice in another campaign.

Approximately 160,000, or 9% of the total inmate population claimed "Complete innocence" and their claims were addressed first, and were posted on the National Registry of Claims of Innocence website, www.registryofclaimsofinnocence.org.

The Commission recommended that where the previously deficient forensic science was an important basis for convictions, those convictions should be set aside and the inmates either be freed or scheduled for a new trial, with or without bail.

Jesus and Jesusa met with a few of the approximately 95,367 inmates who were released from prison in the 2020s and 2030s through the implementation of the Commission's standards.[13] The eradication of wrongful convictions became one of the primary concerns of Jesus and Jesusa, and that concern continued with them for the rest of their lives.

When visiting the State House in Boston in April, they came across the large, but simple, statue of Mary Dyer who was executed by hanging on Boston Common in 1660 for preaching Quakerism, including the view that men and women were equal before God. It was her second conviction and death sentence, but the first was waived in favor of permanent exile. She intentionally returned to Massachusetts to preach and protest. Like all convictions for religious beliefs, and like that for Jesus of Nazareth, Dyer's convictions were wrongful, which made her execution especially heinous.

Said Jesusa to Jesus, "A cousin of the Bush's, Dorothy Bush Rafferty, told me yesterday when I met her at Harvard, that she would give us an introduction to her distant cousin, former Texas Governor Prescott G. Bush. Let's go to Texas and meet him and thank him for leading Texas to abolish the death penalty in 2024. I remember that when he became governor in 2022, he refused to sign any execution warrants, which meant that the infamous Texas count of those executed since 1982 stopped at 629. More importantly, we can seek his assistance for the final stretch of the global campaign to abolish the death penalty."

13. See the National Registry of Exonerations at https://www.law.umich.edu/special/exoneration

The last U.S. state to execute a convicted defendant was Missouri in 2028. After that, it was clear that any future effort to any of the remaining five states with death penalty statutes to actually execute someone would be declared by the U.S. Supreme Court to be "cruel and unusual punishment," which was prohibited by the 8th Amendment to the U.S. Constitution. Except for some rigid literalists in law schools and a few judges, no one interpreted "unusual" to mean infrequent when the 8th amendment was ratified in 1791 with all ten of the first Amendments, also called the "Bill of Rights." Instead, it meant infrequent at the time of the current litigation.

The only remaining countries with the death penalty were Afghanistan, Bangladesh, China, and Iran.

Jesus and Jesusa had known of Bush's efforts since their senior year project at Da Vinci School. Bush was elected as Governor when voters rejected the harsh, vengeful justice approach of the previous governor. Bush campaigned for a "kinder, gentler" Texas, which was a phrase made famous by his grandfather, George H. W. Bush, in his 1988 acceptance speech for the Republican nomination for president when he said, "I want a kinder, gentler nation."

Jesus and Jesusa flew to Texas and met former Governor Prescott Bush at his home, where he explained how he had come to the decision to try to abolish the death penalty. He was brought up as a Roman Catholic and he learned that Pope Ionnes Paulus II had issued an encyclical, "Evangelium Vitae" (The Gospel of Life) in 1995 which stated that capital punishment was appropriate only in cases of absolute necessity, which meant almost never.

As a teenager he had a friend whose father had been sentenced to death for a murder he denied committing. Prescott remembered how the family was preparing for a funeral, when the execution was canceled about 12 hours before the scheduled time. Apparently, a new witness had come forward to say that another man committed the crime and that witness had passed two polygraph examinations. As the other man was in prison for life for other crimes, he agreed that the new witness's story was correct. The bargain was that he would plead guilty to that crime in return for a promise by the state not to seek the death penalty.

Thus, said the ex-governor, "My friend's father was home for Christmas in a car instead of a box."

During the campaign for Governor, Prescott learned that Texas was second only to China in the number of criminals who had been executed since1982, the year that Texas resumed executions after a judicial moratorium. Texas was even "ahead" of Iran and Iraq.

Bush continued, "This second place so-called achievement was not going to help me present Texas to the global investment and business communities as a progressive and modern state. In fact, a global boycott was planned against Texas in 2023 by the World Coalition Against the Death Penalty. My opponent said, 'Go Ahead. Make My Day. Boycott Us,' but the people of Texas didn't agree with that position."

Jesus asked, "Will you join the ongoing effort to persuade China and the other three countries to finally abandon the death penalty. He responded, "Sure. Just tell me what I can do."

They returned home in June 2036 to Salerno for summer vacation. While they were in the U.S., they saw that many Americans still quoted prices in U.S. dollars, even though the mundo was ten years old, and now used by 142 U.N. members. The mundo purchased about what 1.5 dollars used to purchase.

Maria met them at the airport in Napoli. "You both look different," she said. "Did you eat too much American pizza?" That was a family joke, of course. Giuseppe prided himself on his pizza, as did many Italians. That summer the twins worked at the Paestum archeological site as guides. It was an excellent opportunity to continue to learn about the Greek and Roman gods to which the three surviving temples were dedicated. At different times, two of the three temples were built for Hera, the wife and sister of Zeus, head of all the gods. She was the Greek goddess of women, fertility and childbirth.

The apparent dominance of a woman god at Paestum is likely a product of archeology and history. The name "Paestum" is Latin for Posiedon, who was Hera's brother and god of the sea. It's likely that there was a temple to the city's namesake god, even if it hasn't survived or been unearthed.

During that time, Jesus and Jesusa also had time to think about their upcoming studies in China and the potential for their activism there against the death penalty.

That fall, they took the trans-Siberian railway to China for their studies at Beijing University for the 2036-37 academic year. In a sense, the Communist regime since 1949 was a utopian experiment in government without capitalism and private property. Like other utopian communities, it subsequently conformed to the global norms. Five religions were allowed, along with atheism and a Confucian belief system: Taoism, Buddhism, Islam, Protestantism and Catholicism. Beginning in the late 1970's Chinese leaders moved the economy toward capitalism and allowed direct foreign investment. When the controls on the economy were relaxed, the controls on belief systems and religions were also relaxed. By 2040, the Chinese Catholic Church was allowed to re-affiliate itself with the Roman Catholic Church due to changes within China and within the Roman Church.

Jesus and Jesusa soaked up as much as they could about life in China, as the country constituted about 15% of humanity. It was a higher percentage in the late 20th century, but the Chinese leadership realized that population growth was a drag on economic and social growth, rather than an accelerant. With a one-child per family policy, with some exceptions, the Chinese population was stabilized at 1.5 billion in 2028 and it began its decline thereafter.

During the fall, Jesus and Jesusa met with leaders of the China Campaign Against the Death Penalty (CCADP), but were frustrated that there was no concrete plan for action. They had proposed walking atop sections of the Great Wall of China to dramatize the Chinese position as the largest and most frequent user of the death penalty, among the four remaining countries using that punishment for crimes. During the previous decade, China killed an average of 45 of its citizens each year. However, the CCADP voted down the idea, despite some support among the members.

Jesus and Jesusa decided to begin a walk on their own, beginning on Wednesday, February 18, the beginning of the Chinese year 2588. As the year of the Snake, a walk and march along the winding Great Wall seemed symbolic. Jesus and Jesusa would argue to the media, who were certain to come to join their trek, that the Chinese could no more avoid the global movement toward abolition of the death penalty than their Great Wall could keep out invaders – which it didn't.

Jesus and Jesusa took a MAGtrain to Shanhaiguan, where the Great Wall begins at the

Bohai Sea across from Korea,[14] on February 10, and began their blogs on Facebook and Qzone, its Chinese equivalent. Their primary Chinese partner was Zhao Zuohai who had been convicted of murdering a man during a fight in 1998 and was sentenced to death. It was claimed that torture was used to extract his confession. Fortunately, through court appeals, and because the purported death arise from a fight, Zhao Zuohai's sentence was reduced to 29 years.

In 2010, the purported murder victim, Zhenshang Zhao, returned alive to his village and Zhao Zuohai was exonerated, and the inadequacies of the Chinese justice system were exposed. The case bore an uncanny resemblance to the case of the brothers Jesse and Stephen Boorn who were convicted in Vermont, USA for murdering their brother-in-law, Russell Colvin in 1812. The Boorns were convicted and sentenced to hang. Fortunately, appeals took longer than usual, because in 1819, the purported victim was spotted in New Jersey. Colvin was enticed into going to New York City and then tricked into a stagecoach which took him to Vermont instead of his intended return to New Jersey. Upon his arrival in Vermont on December 22, it was clear to waiting observers that he was, in fact, Russell Colvin, and that he was not dead. The hanging of the Boorn brothers, scheduled for January 28, 1820, was canceled.

The Boorn case had been heralded as the first wrongful conviction case in the U.S., but that was unhappily not the case. The brothers were preceded by the convictions and executions of 20 witches in Salem, Massachusetts in1692-93, and the Mary Dyer execution in 1660. There were many more. Nonetheless, the Boorn case was dramatic and the

14. North Korea and South Korea were reunited in 2029, after the death of the last surviving member of the hereditary rulers, the Kim family.

innocence of the brothers was very clear, so the label of "first" stuck.

A major difference between the Zhao Zuohai case and the Boorn brothers was the 190 year interval. When the media learned of Zhao Zuohai's participation in the upcoming march by Jesus and Jesusa, and the U.S.-based media introduced the Boorn case to the news, the embarrassing comparison was presented to the world. Still, China insisted on its right to execute its criminals.

Jesus, Jesusa and Zhao Zuohai started on their trip at "Old Dragon Head" where the Great Wall of China met the Bohai Sea in Shanhaiguan. In the beginning, the media representatives were planning only to meet the marching party in the evenings, when they set up their camp tents. After two days, there were millions of "followers" on Facebook and Qzone, and about 100,000 were joining every few hours. On the third day, the representatives of several media organizations began walking with them, and Chinese citizens joined, too. Some joined for the duration and some joined for a day. Many others brought food and water to the marchers, who completed approximately 25 kilometers a day. At that rate, they would walk the approximately 500 kilometer distance to Mutianyu, about 70 kilometers from Beijing, in about 20 days.

On the 10th day, February 28, Jesus and Jesusa held a media conference, and the world was watching. By this time, Afghanistan and Bangladesh had announced that they were abandoning the using of the death penalty. The leaders of those countries could see the writing on the wall, and neither wanted his/her country to be the last. That dishonor would await either Iran or China.

At the media conference, the CNN reporter asked, "Your blog states that the goal of this march on the Great Wall to Beijing is to bring a global end to the death penalty. Do you think that's realistic?"

Jesusa answered, "We began our march on February 18, and already two of the remaining four countries have finally abandoned the death penalty. As the saying goes, 'Better late than never.' We have approximately ten days to go on this march, and we are down to two countries. We'll see."

The *South China Morning Post* reporter asked, "Are you not afraid that the Chinese government will arrest you?"

Jesus answered, "That would be interesting, wouldn't it? I don't believe we are doing anything wrong." Later, Jesus took the reporter aside for an 'off the record' discussion, and said,.. "Here's the headline around the world, 'China arrests Jesus and Jesusa.' What are they going to do to us, crucify us? They probably would simply put us on a plane, but that would be an act of fear and cowardice. China has for centuries claimed to lead the world with its ethical views. Being the only country, or only one of two countries, to continue a practice roundly condemned by the rest of the world does not sound like leadership to me."

In Iran, there was hope that that country would not be the last. Building on the sharia law custom that the family of a victim can forgive a criminal and thereby lead to a far lesser sentence, if any, the women of the families of the victims of the inmates on death row became re-energized by the Jesus and Jesusa march. The women obtained affidavits from 90% of the families of victims asking that "their" perpetrators be forgiven and not be subjected to the death penalty, i.e. killed. They also ask that the death penalty be abolished entirely in Iran. Like China, Iran was a country that had always aspired to moral leadership, in the Muslim world, and on this issue it was clearly lagging.

On March 1, the Iranian Supreme Leader, Sayyed Ali Khomeini, announced that Iran would no longer execute any criminals. As the number of Iranian executions had declined over the years from 2-300 annually to less than 20 in 2037, the trend toward abolition was being led by the people running the criminal justice system. Clearly, the death penalty was far less acceptable to the people of Iran, especially to young people.

That left China as the holdout, and a classic example of political inertia. Most Chinese opposed the death penalty, and everyone knew that its application had been less frequent since the 2020s, with only 33 executions in 2036, and none of those was in public. However, no Chinese leader wanted to step forward and push the button on this outdated policy. The policy was not only at odds with all of the other members of the United Nations; it also conflicted with other Chinese goals, such as the desire to reunite with Taiwan. Reunification negotiations between the People's Republic of China and Taiwan had begun in 2030, but had stalled on the issue of the death penalty, which Taiwan had abolished in 2021.

The march by Jesus and Jesusa continued to attract Chinese marchers and global interest by all the available broadcast media. On Day 13, Jesus and Jesusa held an impromptu media conference and called on people opposed to the death penalty around the world to march with them. Supporters could show their support by marching around the Chinese embassies in their respective countries. This tactic multiplied the global coverage of the campaign as crowds of over 100,000 encircled 145 Chinese embassies. There was local media coverage at each one, along with 14,500,000 cell phones, tablets and Google glasses.

One Chinese leader had the stature to respond to the invitation by Jesus and Jesusa. That was Sun Sui-Zhang, a great, great granddaughter of the founder of modern China, Sun Yat-Sen. Quietly, she joined the

Jesus and Jesusa march at Simatai and introduced herself to the twins at the end of the day's march.

Sun Sui-Zhang said, "It is an honor to join you, but I fear that if you proceed to Beijing and try to assemble at Tiananmen Square for a rally, you will harden the will of those who resent foreign pressure. The resentment of foreign interference goes far back in Chinese history and is part of our cultural DNA. In fact, the Great Wall itself is a monument to our desire to block foreign intrusion."

Responded Jesusa, "Thank you so much for coming. We, too, are concerned about causing unproductive resistance. How can we negotiate a way forward that respects the will of the world, together with the pride of the Chinese?"

Sun Sui-Zhang was pleased that Jesus and Jesusa were more interested in a peaceful resolution than they were in scoring points or forcing a confrontation at Tiananmen Square. She proposed, "What do you think about this proposal? I will ask the Party leadership to enact a moratorium on executions for six months, while the issue is studied. In return, you would agree to stop your march in Mutianyu, outside Beijing, next week, and ask your supporters around the world to peacefully stop their protests at midnight on March 7th."

Jesus and Jesusa saw merit in the proposal, and the opportunity for both sides to save face and achieve their goals. Sun Sui-Zhang returned to Beijing and secured the agreement of the leadership, and talked by phone with Jesus and Jesusa. The last execution, of a man who had murdered his wife, was on Friday, March 6. The execution was by lethal injection. Sun Sui-Zhang then returned to the Great Wall on March 9 as the 10,000 marchers stopped outside Mutianyu. The next day, Jesus, Jesusa and Sun Sui-Zhang held a media conference to conclude the march, as had been pre-announced around the world.

The Chinese government was true to its word and there were no more executions. Six months later, the formal abolition was announced quietly on the government's website. Henceforth, March 6 was designated as the day of global celebration of the end of the death penalty. The next goal for some forthinkers was the end of killing of all other animals, starting with mammals.

Jesus and Jesusa returned as global heroes to Universitat Heidelberg for the last part of their senior year in May, 2037. Graduation was scheduled for Saturday, August 29 at the Heidelberg campus.

Back in Salerno, early in the summer of 2037, Professor Emeritus Pappalardo, and the two other surviving members of the Salerno fertility team, visited Giuseppe and Maria Prescelto and told them about the origin of their children. From the available information on the internet, Dr. Pappalardo and the team had been watching the development of Jesus and Jesusa. First, of course, they were stunned to see the names that Guiseppe and Maria had given to them – without knowledge of their origin. Second, they were impressed with the twins' spiritual growth. Third, they were concerned about what the knowledge of their origin would do to the twins, their family, and their role in the world.

The fourth issue was the question of publicity. During the 23 years since the births of the twins, there had been several efforts at cloning humans from long dead tissue, but no one had successfully used the technique secretly used by the Salerno team. In fact, the Salerno team had tried to reproduce its own work with other human tissue from deceased members of their own families, but it hadn't worked. Some team members still wondered whether they should have conducted their live experiment, just because they thought they could do it. They wondered why the Jesus and Jesusa project worked, whereas the others did not. Still, the opportunity had arisen in 2013 to change science and the world. Yet the team members were sworn to secrecy, as they agreed, until the twins turned 21 or graduated from college, whichever came later. The team's plan was to write a scholarly paper about what they did, but keep the names of the twins secret, unless the twins agreed. It was a plan that was out of touch with the modern reality of communications, including social networks.

Jesus and Jesusa were coming home before the beginning of the final two month college session in the summer of 2037 and their parents decided that this was the time to tell them about their origin, beyond what they already knew.

The twins knew they were special, but they didn't know why. They used to be the objects of jokes about their names, but they were not the first children to feel the sting of the cruelty of their peers.

Maria began the conversation, "You know, as we have told you, we went to a fertility clinic in order to have children as pregnancy was not coming to us the traditional way – although we had fun trying."

"Yes, Mom," said Jesusa, "but you know how it still embarrasses us to hear about you and Dad having sex. After we were born, that was the last time, right?"

"Ok, good joke," said Guiseppe, "but No. Your mother and I have always had a good sexual relationship. But that's not why we asked you to sit down with us here. We had a visit last week from the medical team at the fertility clinic. They told us who were your real parents, or parent."

"What do you mean, 'or parent' " asked Jesus.

"Well, that's what we're getting to," said Maria. "The DNA of the two eggs which were implanted into my uterus was actually cloned from the body of a single man."

"Wow!" said Jesus, "Why would someone want to do that?"

"Well," said Guiseppe, "because that single man has been dead for 2000 years."

"Like who?" asked Jesusa.

"Like Jesus. That Jesus," responded Maria.

"How could they do that? That's ridiculous. What have you two been smoking or drinking?" said Jesus.

"In a way, I wish that were the explanation, but here's what we were told," said Maria. "Have you ever heard of the 'Foreskin of Calcata' which was purportedly a portion, or entirety of the actual circumcised foreskin of Jesus?"

"No," said both Jesus and Jesusa, and Jesusa continued, "but I just figured it out, as we're familiar with the church relic game."

"Well," said Maria, "before the foreskin disappeared from Calcata in 1983, "a scientist took a sample and brought it to the Universita del Sigli di Salerno for further study and preservation. It was from that sample that the cells were removed and cloned. Originally the idea was somehow to enhance the Catholic Church, but later it became simply a matter of scientific curiosity – to see if it could be done."

"Wow," said the twins in unison.

Said Jesus, "Part of me wishes that you had told us earlier, and part of me wishes that you had never told us."

Jesusa was similarly perplexed, "Now what do we do? This news will either make us circus curiosities or it will give us some gravity to do what we want to do. Maybe this is a blessing."

With their knowledge of religion and of people around the world, Jesus and Jesusa knew that the news of their origin would be of great interest and importance, but they sought to keep it secret, while they had some time to think about it. The four family members agreed to try to keep it secret, but the story was already out of their control.

On August 26, the Salerno team published their article, "Nature-Nurture in Human Cloning," in an academic publication, *The Journal of Human Genetics*. Without giving the names of the twins, the article did speculate about the relative importance of their genes as compared to their upbringing.

The article added new information about the authenticity of the "Holy Prepuce" with carbon-14 analysis. With a margin of error of 50 years, the Salerno team established that the foreskin was 2000 years old, so it could have belonged to Jesus of Nazareth.

One potential problem for the team was the lie that Professor Pappalardo had told Cardinal Donato about the impossibility of the cloning, and the consequent abandonment by the team in 2013 of the foreskin cloning effort. The Cardinal was now deceased and the Salerno team did not know who else in the Vaticano hierarchy knew about the secret effort. The team agreed not to approach the current Vaticano hierarchy about the upcoming article. Because the Church never officially acknowledged that the Vaticano Swiss Guards had taken the foreskin from Calcata in 1983, the origin of the tiny foreskin section which was used to clone Jesus and Jesusa was a delicate matter.

The Salerno team decided to lie again in order to protect themselves and the Vaticano hierarchy from embarrassment. A cover story was invented, which was surely not the first fabrication in the long history of the foreskin of Calcata. The article briefly stated what the team told the Presceltos, which was that Dr. Pappalardo's predecessor at the University had been to Calcata in the early 1980s and had been authorized to cut a section of the foreskin for carbon-14 analysis. The results of that carbon-14 analysis were never revealed, until the current article. When the Pappalardo team found the foreskin section in the laboratory in 2013, they decided to conduct the cloning experiment. The team calculated that the Vaticano would know otherwise, but would be reluctant to officially acknowledge that it had taken the Holy Prepuce from Calcata in 1983. At the time of the burglary, the Vaticano had denied any knowledge of the relic's whereabouts.

When the article was published, so much attention was paid to trying to identify the twins, that the questions about the details of the cutting of the section from the foreskin were not asked.

Despite the team's efforts at anonymity for Jesus and Jesusa, there were calls from journalists to their parents' home on the 27th and to their college dormitory rooms by the 28th. Because the article described the creation of twins of both sexes, and that their names were religion-based, and because it said, "... the twins seem to be endowed with wisdom beyond their years," it wasn't long before the social media focused on Jesus and Jesusa.

The twins knew they had to present the truth, as they knew it, but they begged the reporters for time.

They scheduled a media conference in Salerno for Monday, the 31st and asked reporters not to ask them questions until then. Of course, that didn't prevent the Heidelberg graduation from being one of the most widely publicized college graduations in history. Even without the participation of the twins, the story went viral around the world.

Chapter 5 Coming out and Humanism

At the media conference on Monday, August 31, 2037, the twins began to feel the full impact of who they were and what they represented.

The conference began with Professor Pappalardo describing the work he and his team did to clone cells from the foreskin of Calcata. Two other members of the team were with him, including Allessandro Galvani. No one asked, and Prof. Pappalardo did not explain, when the piece of tissue was lifted from the relic. The relic was famous, but no one compared the year of the birth of Jesus and Jesusa, 2014, with the year, 1983, that the relic was stolen from the home of the priest in Calcata.

"Are you the Second Coming?" asked one reporter. Jesusa responded, "We are here to serve others. As Jesus of Nazareth said, I think it's in Mark, Chapter 10, 'Whoever wants to be a leader among you must be your servant, and whoever wants to be first among you must be the slave of everyone else. For even the Son of Man came not to be served but to serve others and to give his life as a ransom for many.' "

"Which of them was the Messiah?" asked another, to which Jesus answered, "If one of us is, then we both are."

A Muslim reporter asked about their potential roles as Muslim prophets, and Jesusa answered, "We are here for all humanity and all religions. We would be honored if the people of Islam were to consider us to be prophets."

The reporter continued, "But, you are a woman. There are no other women Muslim prophets."

Jesusa was ready, "There were only two women prophets in Judaism and Christianity: Miriam and Deborah, and very few people know anything about them. They were in the past. Whether there were two women prophets in a religion more than a thousand years ago or zero women prophets doesn't seem to make much difference today. We are now in the 21st century, and women are largely free from the shackles of their history. If Islam chooses to reject me because I am a woman, then it will decline further as a religion, just as did the Roman Catholic Church until it opened its doors fully to women. We need to combine the glories of Islam in medieval times when it led the world in science and math, with the need today to embrace men and women equally."

After the media conference, Jesusa said to Jesus, "Did you talk with the members of the medical team, in addition to Professor Pappalardo?"

"Yes," said Jesus, I talked with Dr. Galvani. He seemed very interested in our schooling, our interests and our lives in general."

"Was he the man with the brown hair and short goatee?" asked Jesusa.

"Yes, that was he," answered Jesus.

"Well, did you notice what he looked like?" continued Jesusa.

"What do you mean?" responded Jesus.

"I mean, did you notice that he looked like us?" pressed Jesusa. Did you notice that his eyes were brown. His hair was brown. His nose looked like ours. And so did his unusual ears. His eyebrows were curved like ours and he has a dimple on his cheek."

"Forgive me, Sooz, but last month at the museum in Darmstadt, you looked at the seldom-seen painting, "Arrest of Jesus" by Heinrich Hofmann and you thought that the Jesus in the painting looked like us. And that painting was finished in 1854!"

"Ok. Point taken, but I still think that Prof. Galvani looks like us, or what we will look like in another 25 years. Also, he kept staring at me, and when he wasn't staring at me, he was staring at you. Oh, well."

At age 23, they were not the youngest people to ever experience the thrill and fear of international youthful fame and the temptations and challenges that come with it. Shirley Temple was famous at age five in 1933 and continued to live a productive life. Princess Diana of England struggled with her fame, but morphed into the world's best-known supporter of what became the 1999 International Mine Ban Treaty, before her accidental death in 1997. Austrian Crown Prince Rudolph was heir to the Austro-Hungarian Empire, and all its apparent power and wealth, but he committed suicide at age 31 in 1889. To him and his lover, life was not worth living. The 20th century was littered with rock-and-roll stars who lost their balance and lives quickly, such as Janis Joplin, Jim Morrison, and Michael Jackson in the 21st.

However, Jesus and Jesusa had already developed perspectives on life and humanity and they chose, not unlike some of their peers, to use their fame to change the world for the better. They spoke of peace, and sustainable humanity on Earth, and of the need to severely reduce military budgets. They campaigned for an International Peace Day as part of the general campaign for an International Holiday Treaty. That treaty later became international law in 2040, upon the ratification by 50 countries. Jesus and Jesusa added their voices to the movement to provide family planning services to all men and women around the world in sufficient volume that every child born was a wanted child. While global population growth was slowing down and would soon stabilize, it was still over 8.5 billion.

They visited religious leaders around the world and asked that those leaders encourage their members to seek and find common ground with members of other religions, rather than exploit their differences. They had developed a following, similar to that of the Dalai Lama who, like themselves, was placed by the decisions of others into the forefront of his or her religion.

With all their speaking and traveling, they had little time for their relationships with friends and peers, and thus they had few. It seemed that they were, like their namesake, giving their lives for their fellow humans. They despaired that the human population was destroying their Earth with its fecundity and its toxic gasses and substances.

The burden of their heritage and names haunted them and they decided not to pass that heritage on to others, at least not biologically. Jesus had a vasectomy and Jesusa had a tubal ligation, and they made their decisions public. "It was time," they said, to care about the Earth and for the long term future of humanity." They were not asking, they said, for everyone to have themselves sterilized before having any children, but they recommended the operation for all who had made that decision, with or without children.

The major religions of the world took notice of these courageous twins, for they understood the meaning of sacrifice, and sacrifice was part of the core of those religions. Now, the questions came more frequently from the Jews, "Are you the messiahs?" And from the Christians, "Are you the Second Coming of Christ?" Such questions and hyperbole annoyed Jesus and Jesusa because they focused on their perceived divinity rather than their ideas.

However, like others born into outsized roles, such as the heirs to the British crown, they understood the reality of their fame. They knew that scientists created their first cells from the skin tissue of a long-long-deceased human who most likely was not the man called Jesus of Nazareth. They also knew that the primary reason that anyone listened to them was because, like their namesake, of the claims of their unusual births. It was a dilemma of dilemmas.

They knew they loved each other, but they kept that physical relationship secret and infrequent. When traveling together, they always had separate rooms. They thought that the public would never tolerate their sexual relationship. They knew that incest was prohibited in civilized societies as a pre-modern way to prevent unwanted genetic mutations. However, even though their sterilizations doubly assured the prevention of such mutations, the taboo was too strong to test openly.

Jesus found himself to be part asexual and part bisexual. He had quiet relationships with men and women, but his closest friends knew that his first love was for his sister. Similarly, Jesusa was bisexual, but mostly loved women, except for Jesus.

As their fame and influence spread, they understood that it was not what their namesake said and did that led to the creation of a religion in his name. It was the mythology of who he was and what his followers, especially Paul, said about him after his crucifixion. Further, it was his sacrifice and the sacrifices of his followers which gave momentum to Christianity.

Jesus and Jesusa looked for the best opportunity for their unique voice. At an environmental conference in Istanbul in May 2038, they met the former leader of the International Humanist and Ethical Union (IHEU), Sonja Eggerickx, and they explored their mutual interests. She encouraged Jesus and Jesusa to join and take a leadership role in the IHEU. Jesus and Jesusa wanted people to focus on Earth-oriented values and discard the mythology in many religions of where founders of religions came from, or where their bodies went after death. To them, fertilized eggs become embryos in mothers' bodies and people are born, and when they die, their bodies are all that remain, and not for long.

"In this respect," they would say, "we are no different from the other mammals on this earth." Further, they would remind their audiences, "From dust unto dust..."

They knew about the IHEU from their studies and they remembered learning that the brother of Aldous Huxley, author of the dystopian novel, *Brave New World*, was Julian Huxley who was one of the founders of the IHEU. The Huxley family was distinguished for many reasons, and the brothers were the grandsons of Thomas Henry Huxley, a friend and supporter of Charles Darwin.

In the fall of 2038, Jesus and Jesusa were elected co-presidents of the IHEU and the organization prospered. Many new members cited the "children of Jesus" as the reason for their support of humanism. "If a child of Jesus can dismantle the mythology of Jesus's purported birth and death, then it's safe for all of us," wrote one new member on an IHEU blog.

As Jesus and Jesusa were seeking to promote a better life for all humans on earth, their earlier interest in utopias blossomed into support for advocates of a future, more rational society. They joined in the endorsement of the "Great Transformation," the 50-year campaign which was announced in 2020. The number of people who openly declared themselves to be atheists or humanists grew dramatically after their election.

One of the co-presidents' first priorities was to seek out other organizations and religions and find common beliefs and philosophies with them. They chose, however, to stay with traditional humanism rather than extending the philosophy to transhumanism, which was the belief that with science and technology the abilities of humans could be expanded beyond the norm. A founder of transhumanism was the same Julian Huxley who helped found humanism. He wrote in 1957, "The human species can, if it wishes, transcend itself - not just sporadically, an individual here in one way, an individual there in another way, but in its entirety, as humanity."[1] Jesus and Jesusa believed that while the elites and wealthy of the world could avail themselves of the genetic technology to lengthen their lives and to expand the powers of their minds, such efforts could not be endorsed while there was no feasible way to extend those benefits to everyone.

The beliefs of the members of the IHEU were summarized in its 2002 "Amsterdam Declaration,"[2] as subsequently modified by the 2018 Geneva Declaration which eliminated references to established religions. Written in "British English," it states:

Humanism is the outcome of a long tradition of free thought that has inspired many of the world's great thinkers and creative artists and gave rise to science itself.

The fundamentals of modern Humanism are as follows:

1. Humanism is ethical. It affirms the worth, dignity and autonomy of the individual and the right of every human being to the greatest possible freedom compatible with the rights of others. Humanists have a duty of care to all of humanity including future generations. Humanists believe that morality is an intrinsic part of human nature based on understanding and a concern for others, needing no external sanction.

2. Humanism is rational. It seeks to use science creatively, not destructively. Humanists believe that the solutions to the world's problems lie in human thought and action. Humanists believe that science rather than belief will uncover the truths about the origins of our

---

1. Julian Huxley, *In Bottles for New Wine*, 1957, at http://www.transhumanism.org/index.php/WTA/more/huxley/
2. See the IHEU website, http://iheu.org/humanism/the-amsterdam-declaration/

universe and life on earth. Humanism advocates the application of the methods of science and free inquiry to the problems of human welfare. But Humanists also believe that the application of science and technology must be tempered by human values. Science gives us the means but human values must propose the ends.

3. Humanism supports democracy and human rights. Humanism aims at the fullest possible development of every human being. It holds that democracy and human development are matters of right. The principles of democracy and human rights can be applied to many human relationships and are not restricted to methods of government.

4. Humanism insists that personal liberty must be combined with social responsibility. Humanism ventures to build a world on the idea of the free person responsible to society, and recognises our dependence on and responsibility for the natural world. Humanism is undogmatic, imposing no creed upon its adherents. It is thus committed to education free from indoctrination.

5. Humanism recognises that reliable knowledge of the world and ourselves arises through a continuing process of observation, evaluation and revision.

6. Humanism values artistic creativity and imagination and recognises the transforming power of art. Humanism affirms the importance of literature, music, and the visual and performing arts for personal development and fulfilment.

7. Humanism is a lifestance aiming at the maximum possible fulfilment through the cultivation of ethical and creative living and offers an ethical and rational means of addressing the challenges of our times. Humanism can be a way of life for everyone everywhere.

8. Humanists recognise the rights of other animal species to live as they have evolved without human predation. While understanding that humans ate other animals for centuries, humanists seek a return to vegan diets for themselves and the world. Humanists support the extension of the imperative "thou shall not kill," to all animals, except where necessity requires.

Our primary task is to make human beings aware in the simplest terms of what Humanism can mean to them and what it commits them to. By utilising free inquiry, the power of science and creative imagination for the furtherance of peace and in the service of compassion, Humanists have confidence that people have the means to solve the earth's problems.

Paragraph 8 was added at Geneva in recognition of the increased understanding that humans are one animal species among many and that humans deserve no special rights or privileges. Humans were never, by nature, predators, and they should return to their original sources of food for their own benefit and the improved welfare of the Earth and its other animal species.

In 2039 Jesus and Jesusa circulated these principles to the leaders of all major religions and asked, rhetorically, "Are we not all humanists?" They asked for comments and contributions for a new IHEU declaration of principles. They asked, "Please tell us what parts of this declaration conflicts with the principles of your religion, and secondly, what you would add." The final result was the 2041 Global Religious Framework which began with the "basic statement" of human ethical and moral beliefs followed by 26 appendices where each of the major religions presented what was unique about that religion and which was not accepted into the "basic statement."

Chapter 6 Co-Popes in the Church

In January, 2039, Jesus and Jesusa met with Pope Francesco II, who succeeded to the papacy in 2027 after the abdication of Pope Francesco, now called Pope Francesco I, on his birthday, December 17, 2026 at the age of 90. Formerly called Cardinal Agapiti Ndimbo, Pope Francesco II was from Tanzania and was the first Black pope.

"Welcome to the Vaticano," said the Pope. "We have much to talk about."

"Thank you very much," said Jesus and Jesusa, together. "We've been looking forward to this day," continued Jesusa, "for several years."

"What can we do, together, to serve humanity?" asked Jesus.

If Pope Francesco II knew anything about the actual source of the cloned section of the Holy Prepuce, he said nothing to Jesus and Jesusa. They, in turn, knew nothing more than what was said at the 2037 press conference and in the article by Professor Pappalardo and his team.

The Pope told them of his plan to convene a Vaticano Council IV in 2042, 20 years after the convening of the reform Vaticano Council III, which had endorsed the ordination of women, the abandonment of celibacy and the welcoming of marriage for all priests.

He then interrupted himself, "Before I continue with the planned changes in the church," he said, "I want to hear about your views on the moral issues relating to human food consumption."

Jesusa responded for herself and Jesus, as this was one of her areas of specialization, "Ok. I'll start. For the next two or three hundred years, until the human population returns to an equilibrium or sustainable level of one or two billion, we have to reduce our ecological burden on the Earth. One way is to eat foods lower on the food chain. For example, a single hectare[1] of land planted with potatoes can feed 29 people for a year. However, if that same hectare is planted with grass for cattle, the resulting meat will feed only one person for a year. If sheep are the grazing animals, there will be meat for two people. You can see how the eating of meat consumes at least ten times as much land as the eating of grains and vegetables. Of course, there are variations by country and continent and by level of economic development. We cannot develop any scale of morality that favors the rich, who have been the people historically who could afford to eat meat."

"Agreed," said Pope Francesco II. "It's been generally forgotten that we ask Catholics to abstain from eating meat on Fridays, in deference to the memory of the death of Jesus of Nazareth on Good Friday. What we could do is remind Catholics of that request for abstinence and ask that they abstain from eating both meat and fish on two other days a week, as a means of respecting the animals which support us on the other days. It also shows respect for our Earth. Someday we can ask people to live without meat and fish every day of every week, but we must pace ourselves."

"That's excellent," answered Jesus. "If all Catholics, and an equal number of non-Catholic Christians and Humanists responded to your requests, the reduction of meat consumption would achieve three goals. First, it would permit those who needed to eat more meat-based protein, but for whom supplies were costly and limited, to eat that meat. Second, it would reduce the pressure to use increasing amounts of land for grazing of animals for food. Third, it would

1. A hectare contains 10,000 square meters and typically measures 100 meters by 100 meters. It is equivalent to 2.47 acres.

decrease, or at least not lead to further increases of, greenhouse gasses, including methanol, from the animals' waste products."

Continued Jesusa, "Our goal is to gradually eliminate the consumption of meat and fish that requires the killing of animals. While some vegan purists also do not eat products of animals, primarily milk products such as milk, cheese, and butter, we don't think it's necessary or feasible to go that far. The key is that we believe we can respect and care for animals while still eating their eggs and their milk products.

The sheer scale of the killing of animals for food is breathtaking – pardon the pun. Approximately 20 billion chickens and 250 million cattle, 700 million pigs, and millions of ducks, goats, and sheep are killed every year for meat. That carnage should decline dramatically, and finally stop. Putting it in human per capita terms, on average each North American and Western European killed and ate approximately 30 animals last year, and that doesn't count the fish. Actually, the lives of fish are so minimized in our civilization that they are not individually counted by anyone except the sportsfishing people. Their killing of fish by painfully hooking their mouths onto bait, which is often composed of dead fish, is even more hideous than killing them for food.[2] Fish do have brains and they do feel pain.

It's not that eating meat and fish has always been wrong. There certainly were times when humans needed to eat meat, either from hunting or fishing, or from domesticated animals. Now, however, in the 22nd century, most humans do not need to eat meat because their essential nutrition is available from the

---

2. The slogan of the Fish Liberation Organization (FLO) was "Let's get fish off the hook." See www.flo.com. [As of 2014, not a real website.]

other food groups, and from our manufactured a-food; and that's what tips the scale in favor of vegetarianism.

It was once thought that animal protein was necessary for an active human life, but nutrition science proved that to be wrong. Many famous people, including athletes, have been vegetarians. They include Christine Lagarde, who helped bring the world to a Single Global Currency, Leonardo da Vinci, Steve Jobs, Martina Navratilova, and Albert Einstein. Your predecessor, Pope Francesco I became a vegetarian, even though he was from the beef eating and beef producing country of Argentina.

We ask that you declare not that it's immoral to eat meat, at least not yet, but that one core of our morality is the preservation of the Earth, and the moral course of action is to reduce the eating of meat."

The Pope agreed, "Our church used to have absolute rules. This sounds more like 'moral relativity.' You can be good if you reduce your meat consumption. You can be better in the eyes of the Church if you eliminate meat consumption. Few of us can be perfect, but we can try to get as close as we can."

Moving beyond the subject of food, Pope Francesco II was planning to recommend the de-mythologization of the Catholic Church, meaning that the Church would abandon the long-held views in such impossible myths as the virgin birth of Jesus of Nazareth, his ascension into a heaven that does not exist for him or anyone else, and the existence of a personal God. Also to be abandoned were the claimed miracles of Jesus of Nazareth and some of his followers.

Said Pope Francesco, "Jesus of Nazareth was a wonderful man," but he didn't restore Lazarus or anyone else from the dead, and he didn't walk on water. Instead," the Pope continued, "I will urge the Church to focus its mission on what Jesus of Nazareth actually said and did as a human being." The messages of love and forgiveness from Jesus of Nazareth were especially important to Pope Francesco. For these dramatic changes he believed he had the support of most of the Cardinals, especially, of course, from those he had most recently appointed.

The pope said, "The Golden Rule seems a good place to start. Jesus said, 'Do to others whatever you would like them to do to you. This is the essence of all that is taught in the law and the prophets.'[3]"

Jesusa responded, "We agree. And what's incredible is that the Golden Rule is part of the philosophy of almost every religion and non-religious values groups. There are similar texts in Confucianism, Buddhism, Judaism, Islam, ancient Roma, ancient Graecia, Hinduism, you name it."

The Pope continued, "One of my favorite messages from Jesus - not you, of course, the first one - is about the need to seek truth. I recall from my seminary days learning that Jesus urged his followers, 'And so I tell you, keep on asking, and you will receive what you ask for. Keep on seeking, and you will find. Keep on knocking, and the door will be opened to you. For everyone who asks, receives. Everyone who seeks, finds. And to everyone who knocks, the door will be opened.'[4] And, of course, 'the truth shall set you free.'[5] "

Despite the ordination of women, the population of the Catholic Church was continuing its long decline, as education in sciences continued to grow. Polls had shown to Pope Francesco II that former Catholics and potential Catholics viewed the myths of the traditional Church as the barriers to their future religious participation. Most of the new women priests and

3. Book of Matthew 7:12
4. Book of Luke 11:9-10
5. Book of John 8:32

bishops and supported this de-mytholization change, and they were lobbying their cardinal superiors.

"Let's talk," said the Pope, "about your interest in joining the priesthood of the Catholic Church."

"Yes," said Jesus, "we've thought for a long time that we belong in the Catholic Church, given the special circumstances of our births. As co-presidents of the IHEU, we can communicate the messages of Jesus of Nazareth, although we present them in humanist ways. If we were simultaneously officers of the Church, we believe our messages could be more powerful and authentic."

"Of course," replied Pope Francesco II, "it would be a novel step to instantaneously pronounce you as priests, and not everyone in the hierarchy would approve. However, we must take innovative steps if we are to stay relevant, and move humanity in the right direction."

"I just remembered," recalled Pope Francesco II. "One ironic item to discuss is the circumstance of your own birth. Some people believe that you are both the children of Jesus of Nazareth. Should that claim be added to the myths which the Church is about to abandon?"

Jesus responded, "That's a good question. Jesusa and I have always wondered about our birth. As Winston Churchill said about the circumstances of his own birth, when he was born eight months after the marriage of his parents, Lord Randolph Churchill and Jennie Jerome Churchill, 'Although present on the occasion, I have no clear recollection of the events leading up to it.' In other words, we are not responsible for the information about our births. We have always minimized the idea of the cloning from the 'Holy Prepuce' relice, and surmised that someone was mistaken about some aspect of the story, but we never launched our own investigation to explore the truth."

"Right," affirmed Jesusa. "As we never claimed parentage from Jesus of Nazareth, we never were part of our parents' story. Like Churchill, we were not in a position to affirm or deny the story. We've been skeptical, like most people. We've been reluctant to call it a myth, during our parents' lifetime, as it was what they were told and no one has totally disproved the idea. I think that Churchill's position was correct. Let's set aside the story with humor and a dose of skepticism."

"I agree," said Pope Francesco. "My staff thought this might be a problem for me and you, but I don't think so."

At the conclusion of their visit, Pope Francesco II announced to the media in the press room the simultaneous ordination of Jesus and Jesusa as Catholic priests, together with their immediate elevation as cardinals. Jesusa thus became the sixth woman Catholic Cardinal.

Pope Francesco II immediately addressed the question about Jesus and Jesusa that journalists and some cardinals, bishops and priests were likely to ask, which was, "What about the origin of Jesus and Jesusa? Was that a myth, too?" With the prior approval of Jesus and Jesusa, after their quiet discussion earlier in the day, Pope Francesco II said that the foreskin of Calcata was most certainly not a fragment of the body of Jesus of Nazareth. This myth, like so many others in the Church, needed to be cast away and replaced with reality. He then added the obvious, which was that Jesus and Jesusa were not in any way related to Jesus of Nazareth – except one, which was that they were almost divine people, and the Church was honored to have them.

The Pope explained how the IHEU and the Catholic Church would be working together over the next three years to promote their mutual interests. By this time the IHEU claimed over two billion members or passive sympathizers, which put it at about the same size as all of Christianity. For the Catholic Church to align with such a large group would help the Church survive into the next centuries.

Combining their roles as co-presidents of the IHEU and as Cardinals of the Church, Jesus and Jesusa reached out to the Jews of the world and traveled to Israel and other Jewish centers. They actively, but quietly, sought recognition as messiahs, but that was not yet attainable. Since ancient times, many men and one woman, Eve Frank, 1754-1816, sought recognition as the Messiah who would usher in a new era of justice, peace and plenty. In short, a Messiah would transform the lot of humanity, or the Jewish people at least, into a real utopia. Aside from earning a Wikipedia entry to the List of "Jewish Messiah Claimants," Jesus and Jesusa did not make much progress.

Similarly they went to Medina and Mecca and sought the support of Islamic leaders for both of them to be recognized as prophets in the Muslim faith, just as Jesus of Nazareth was recognized as an Islamic prophet.

In 2042, Jesus and Jesusa joined other Cardinals at the Vatican Council IV and lobbied their peer Cardinals to join in declarations that the source of Christian faith was not in the divinity of Christ, just as they were not divine, but in the messages that he left with his disciples.

In 2043, the Vatican Council IV released its determinations, the most important of which was the de-mytholization of Catholicism. The Catholic Church was to be a humanist church. There were dissenters, to be sure, but now the Church would move forward to assist its members in the real moral issues of the day which related to the care of the Earth and the need to reduce the size of the human population, and increase the spiritual and physical welfare of all.

Supporting that focus on the true moral issues facing humanity, the Vaticano Council IV endorsed Pope Francesco II's proposal for the Vaticano to abandon its status as a political unit. There was no modern reason for the Catholic Church to be the only religion in the world which also was a political state. The change meant large financial savings for the dismantling of the Vaticano diplomatic corps, including its mission to the United Nations. Instead of being a state, the territory of the Vaticano would be included within Municipio I, one of the 15 municipalities of the City of Roma. The approximately 900 citizens of the Vaticano City became citizens of Roma and Italia. A pope had one vote, like every other citizen of Roma, and s/he could run for City Council or Mayor if s/he chose. These changes were subsequently negotiated with the Government of Italia as amendments to the 1929 Lateran Treaty. This change was not as radical as might have seemed to those without more knowledge of Italian history. After the formation of the modern Italian state in the mid-19th century, the Papal States ceased to exist and the pope had no temporal authority from 1870 to 1929. At that latter date, Dictator Benito Mussolini negotiated the Lateran Treaty to settle the long simmering dispute between Italia and the Church. Thus, the abolition of the Vaticano state meant a return to the status quo from 1870 to 1929.

Pursuant to the Council's determination, Pope Francesco II announced that the Catholic Church would be formally joining the IHEU.

He also announced his intention to abdicate in 2044 and retire to a monastery in Tanzania, where he could pray for the return of the snows to Mt. Kilimanjaro. He took the unusual step of designating Jesus and Jesusa as his nominees to become co-popes. He expected the College of Cardinals to convene later that year to confirm his selections.

That fall, the College convened at the Vaticano. Pope Francesco reaffirmed his earlier announcement and told the conclave that he planned to abdicate, but that he would not do so unless the Cardinals agreed by sacred pledge to elect Jesus and Jesusa as co-popes. There was considerable debate, the content of which leaked to the public, despite efforts to keep it secret. The conservatives wanted a man to become the next pope, and then to roll back the reforms of Vatican Council III. The liberals saw that the downward sprial of the population of the Catholic Church would continue if their theology continued to sponsor myths as real and as a core of religious belief. They also supported the change in the political status of the Vaticano. They reminded the conservatives of the words of Jesus of Nazareth, "Render unto Caesar the things that are Caesar's, and unto God the things that are God's."

Finally, the Cardinals acceded to Pope Francesco II's wishes. The white smoke was sent up the chimney, but for the first time it was not created by fire. It would have been easy to get a permit to have a small fire to create the traditional white smoke, formerly with dry straw together with the used paper ballots, but now with chemicals. Instead, Pope Francesco II decided to have the white smoke created entirely by electricity, using the technology of electronic cigarettes which were banned worldwide in 2025. The black smoke, generated for the previous votes to indicate an inconclusive balloting, was also created electronically.

Jesus and Jesusa thus became on October 15, 2044, the first co-popes, and Jesusa was the first woman pope. Also, at age 30, they were the youngest popes in modern church history, since the papacy of Pope Ionnes XII who became pope at the age of 18 in 955 A.D.

Breaking with recent history in many ways, Jesus and Jesusa chose to keep their names and administer the Church as Co-Pope Jesus and Co-Pope Jesusa. The last pope to keep his name upon elevation to the papacy was Pope Hadrianus VI, 1522-1523, who was born in Holland as Adriaan (the Dutch equivalent of Hadrianus) Floriszoon Boeyens. That was more than 500 years earlier, and the next most recent was 500 years before that, when Giovanni (the Italian equivalent of Ioannes, or John in English) Fasano Phasianus became Pope Iohannes XVIII from 1003 to 1009. The first pope to change his name upon his elevation to that office was a Roman named Mercurio who became Pope Iohannes II in 533.

The tradition of changing one's name when becoming pope was analogous to the Western tradition, particularly in the U.K. and U.S., of a woman changing her surname to her husband's upon marriage. That tradition was almost completely abandoned by the late 21st century. In the Catholic Church popes were thought to be married to the church, hence the practice of changing their names.

Chapter 7 World Tour and Common Ground

In May of 2045, the Co-Popes began a world tour going eastward, beginning with Istanbul. There, they signed an agreement authorizing the mutual exploration of re-unification of the Roman Catholic Church with the Eastern Orthodox Church, from which it split in 1054. The agreement specifically set 2054 as the target date for re-unification, which would mark the end of the 1,000 year schism. This agreement was a followup to the historic meeting in 1964 between Pope Paulus VI and Ecumenical Patriarch Athenagoras in Jerusalem. That led to the Pope's rescission of the excommunications which were ordered in 1054 by Pope Leo IX.

Jesus and Jesusa then traveled to Jerusalem, but via an indirect route. They first took a MAGtrain to Aleppo, Syria, and then a car to the three peaks of Mount Hermon, a symbol of the earlier divisions and wars among the Syrians, Lebanese and Israelis. Thanks to the 2021 Alexandria Treaty among the Israelis and their Muslim neighbors, Mount Hermon and the Golan Heights had been returned to full Syrian sovereignty, except that its military was not allowed in the territory.

The Alexandria Treaty was a long time in coming, if one considers the 1967 U.N. Resolution 242, or even Resolution 394 of 1950, as the beginning of negotiations. The basic formula was that Israel returned nearly all of the West Bank and all of Gaza to the Palestinian State in return for Palestinian recognition of Israel. Many of the illegal Israeli settlements in the West Bank were simply acknowledged to be entirely within, and governed, by Palestine. After considerable education and public relations by the Palestine government, the Jews in those settlements were persuaded that the Palestinian laws were fair and that they would be fairly

administered, regardless of religious orientation, as
was required in the Alexandria Treaty. An added
incentive to accepting Palestinian citizenship and
authority was that the Palestinian tax rates were
substantially lower than in Israel. A few of the larger
settlements and those close to Jerusalem were
determined to be subject to Palestinian property and
commercial law, but their residents were dual citizens
of Israel and Palestine with respect to civil liberties.
Each country was free to establish its capital wherever
it wished and each country was required to protect the
religious freedom of its citizens.

A relatively new issue for the Israelis and
Palestinians was the abolition of the Israeli nuclear
weapons program. This became feasible after Iran
agreed in 2015 to stop entirely its nuclear energy
program which could relate to military use. Pursuant
to the Alexandria Treaty, Israel then became nuclear-
free, just as had been achieved in South Africa in
1989, when that country's government was persuaded
to abandon its program, which had already produced
several atomic bombs. In 2003, Libya voluntarily
renounced its nuclear weapons program. In return for
Israel's abandonment of its nuclear weapons, the
military budgets of its neighboring countries were
slashed.

From Mt. Hermon, the Co-Popes walked the
approximately 320 kilometers to Jerusalem, stopping
at sites along the way where Jesus and several
prophets of Islam had preached. They walked along
the Jordan River and swam in the Sea of Galilee.
Arriving in Jerusalem they spent an equal amount of
time at Christian, Jewish and Muslim holy sites and in
meetings with the leaders of the three faiths.

At the Temple Mount, a place holy to the three
faiths, the Co-Popes signed an accord with several
Jewish and Muslim leaders. There were only 15 million

Jews in the world,[1] but Israel was primarily a Jewish country and the Temple Mount was in Israel. The Jews were represented by leaders of the Conservative, Orthodox and Reform branches, with the Reform leader coming from the United States.

Representing Islam were four Sunni leaders from Indonesia, Nigeria, Pakistan and Saudi Arabia and one Shia leader from Iran. Since 2042, approximately 1,400 years after the beginning of the Sunni/Shia schism which began in the leadership struggle after the death of the prophet Muhammed in 632, these leaders and about 20 others had been negotiating in Mecca to end that schism. Jesus and Jesusa encouraged the Muslim leaders at Temple Mount to continue those negotiations and come to an agreement, just as the leaders of Christianity had done. The perils facing the Earth were too great to waste time and energy in divisive theology, based on differences among Muhammed's successors so long ago.

Another reason for the two Muslim denominations to merge was that the rapid growth of the early 21st century had stopped and reversed, primarily due to the perception that Islam was hostile to women. The "honor killings" were primarily of women whose only crime was love for a man, and much less frequently a woman, they loved in preference to the persons chosen for them by their families. There were an estimated 8,000 such killings in 2010, but the publicity generated by the increasingly universal social media, caused widespread revulsion at the practice and at Islam in general. By unifying the two major denominations, their leaders hoped to show that the

---

[1]. Before six million Jews were murdered in the World War II holocaust, the global Jewish population was approximately 15.5 million, of whom 9.6 million lived in Europe. Thus, the holocaust saw the loss of 39% of the world Jewish population and 63% of the European Jewish population.

way forward was through reasonable discussion rather than hatred of those with whom there were disagreements.

Also invited and signing to the Temple Mount signing were the leaders of the ten largest Christian denominations, including the Eastern Orthodox, Protestants and Anglicans. Based on the 2041 Global Religious Framework, the accord presented the goal of merging their faiths into a single faith based not on the divinity of any of their ancestor leaders, but on the views of humanity they held in common. The Accord, later known as the Temple Mount Accord of 2045 also expressed a desire to join with the faiths of Asia and Africa and with interested secular humanists. It is presented below:

> We leaders of several religious faiths proclaim our mutual interest in bringing humanity together toward several common beliefs:
>
> 1. Our religions arose from times when little was known about ourselves and about our universe.
> 2. The world now faces unprecedented environmental challenges which we must face together.
> 3. We share common values of justice, social justice, fostering community, kindness, trust, and curiosity.
> 4. We shall work together to discourage violence and injustice as actions incompatible with our shared understanding of religion.
> 5. Our differences, and the differences among our members and fellow citizens must be resolved through discussion and dialogue, rather than hostility and violence. Where there are differences which cannot

be yet resolved, and which do not conflict with our common values, we pledge to set those aside and not permit them to interfere with those common values and interests.

6. We call for a global religious enclave to be held in 2047 to reach further understanding or our common beliefs and interests, for the benefit of our members or congregants. The primary goal of that enclave would be establish a global common core of beliefs which all humanity could share, while simultaneously maintaining local traditions which are not in conflict.

Jesusa said at the media conference afterwards, "When Jesus of Nazareth said, 'Every kingdom divided against itself is brought to desolation; and every city or house divided against itself shall not stand,'[2] he could have been speaking to us today. We humans must overcome the divisions among us, and together protect our Earth."

One result of these efforts to bridge the gaps among religions was the near elimination of sectarian violence within the Muslim world, and from that world toward the Western world. The other contributing factor was the dramatic reduction in population growth, which, in turn, reduced the previously large numbers of unemployed or underemployed young and disaffected Muslim men. Further, the increased equality of Muslim women led to more open expressions of sexuality which had been repressed in that religion for hundreds of years. That change, too,

2. Book of Matthew, 12:25.

further reduced the frustrations of Muslim men which previously were directed at Westerners and women.

They then went to Kahuta, Pakistan to bring a message of peace to the survivors of the 2020 nuclear explosion. The twins were six years old when the world suffered its third atomic bomb explosion in a populated area. Over 80,000 people were killed, and another 90,000 were seriously injured. Kahuta was one of Pakistan's nuclear weapon development sites, and scientists later determined that the explosion was an accident due to a timing device that was erroneously activated. At least that is what the Pakistanis said. In fact, it may have been that the bomb exploded when someone was trying to steal it. In any case, it was another painful reminder that the Earth needed to rid itself of nuclear weapons.

Learning about the 2020 Kahuta bomb when Jesus and Jesusa were at the Da Vinci School had a significant effect on their decisions to work for world peace and religious tolerance and unity for the rest of their lives.

At Kahuta, they visited tombs of the thousands of unknown dead and visited with the survivors of the explosion which was only 25 years earlier.

Continuing eastward, the Co-Popes flew to India and met with Hindu leaders. They bathed in the Ganges River, which fortunately had been substantially cleaned up since it had been classified in the early 2000s as one of the world's most polluted rivers. They witnessed a solar cremation at one of the country's 23,000 solar crematoria. The use of these crematoria was credited with contributing to the reversal of Indian deforestation and the slow restoration of India's forests. Prior to the "Great Transformation," cremation was not favored by several religions, including the Baha'i's, but the Hindus led the world toward making the practice nearly universal. The next most popular means of disposing of the bodies of the dead was to bury them, without protection from solid materials, so their bodies would decay into the soil and thus regenerate in future plants and animals.

Jesus and Jesusa visited 'Sabarati Ashram,' one of the homes of Mahatma Gandhi, whose life work they had studied during their Johannesburg college year in 2034-35. Now, they were especially interested in his, and Hindu, respect for animals. They had read the famous quote, though incorrectly attributed to Gandhi, "The greatness of a nation and its moral progress can be judged by the way its animals are treated."[3] They had supported the "Respect Animals Movement" (RAM) and had long ago stopped eating meat and fish.

In a light moment, the twins were presented sets of ten Nehru shirts with their trademark short upright collars, which were similar to the collarless shirts which Jesus and Jesusa favored since their "Cotton Revolution" back at Da Vinci School.

Next, Jesus and Jesusa flew to Thailand to meet with Southeast Asian Buddhist leaders. "We must do what we can to save humanity," said Jesusa, "and working together with a common spiritual vision will help all of us do that work." The Buddhist leaders expressed optimism that the 2047 global conclave would be successful.

For Jesus and Jesusa, traveling to Beijing was a return "home" as they had spent almost a year there as students, and activists against the death penalty.

---

3. This was one of many times in which wise statements were attributed to people, but for which there was no reliable source. Others who denied making widely quoted statements attributed to them were Senator Everett Dirksen ("A billion here, a billion there, and pretty soon you're talking about real money.") and Margaret Mead, ("Never doubt that a small group of thoughtful, committed citizens can change the world; indeed, it's the only thing that ever has.") and William Sutton, ("I rob banks because that's where the money is.")

The Communist Party was no longer the only political party, as the country's politics had evolved into a multi-party system. Nonetheless, atheism was still more of an official religion than in any other country, although it had substantially evolved into humanism. Jesus and Jesusa assured their Chinese hosts, "We look forward to talking to everyone here, including atheists and humanists. If atheists care enough about their belief system to label themselves in some way, then they must have come to some recognition of their values, and we can talk."

Next, they flew to Lima, Peru and visited the major countries of South America traveling south along the Pacific coast and then back north along the Atlantic, and then to Cuba. South America still had the largest percentage Catholic population of any of the continents. From Beijing, they had considered going from Beijing to North America via the China-TransSiberian-Alaska MAGtrain, which was just completed in 2039, but that route took them too far out of their way.

Cuba was a special destination because of the powerful example of reconciliation between that country and the United States. In 2034, the United States unilaterally announced that it was giving up its perpetual 100-year old lease of the 116.5 square kilometer Guantanamo Naval Base, which had also been the site of the notorious prison camps for alleged Muslim fighters after September 11, 2001. In 2018, after the departure from the Cuban government of Raul and Fidel Castro, normal diplomatic and commercial relations were established between Cuba and the United States, including the payment of compensation for private property expropriated in 1959. The restoration of the Guantanamo base to Cuba capped 16 years of increasingly cordial relations.

In Havana, Jesus and Jesusa dedicated the renovated Havana Cathedral of Mother Mary, formerly called the Cathedral of the Virgin Mary. As with other churches and places with references to the now-discarded myth of a virgin birth, the name of the Havana Cathedral was changed. The mother of Jesus of Nazareth was still much revered in the Catholic Church for the values that she instilled in her son, but most Christian churches followed the lead of the Roman Catholic Church which proclaimed at its Vaticano Council IV that it no longer needed to rely upon myths for its spiritual strength.

Before heading to Western Europe and Roma, the Co-Popes flew to Miami for a New Year's Eve celebration and Mass. The Church continued the rituals of Mass with the sharing of bread and wine as symbols of the bodily and spiritual sharing of the sustenance for humanity.

Not everyone in the Catholic Church welcomed the changes brought by Vaticano Councils III and IV and by the ascendancy of Co-Popes Jesus and Jesusa. Before the trip began, Church leaders in the U.S. advised against coming to the U.S. for fear of an assassination attempt by disgruntled Catholics or from anyone who disapproved of the Co-Popes, or their presumed sexuality or their views. Too many such people still had weapons. There was some relief when the trip to Miami concluded without serious incident, aside from some heckling and threatening words on the Internet. "See," said Jesus to Jesusa, "despite some bitterness in the U.S. about its relative decline in the world, and despite some Catholic opposition to what we have done and what we symbolize, our messages of love and optimism are still welcome here." Officials in Dallas cringed when they heard of that comment, with its echo of the 1963 statement by Mrs. Connolly, the Texas governor's wife, to John Kennedy just before her husband and President Kennedy were shot, "Mr. President, you cannot say that Dallas doesn't love you."

As children, Jesus and Jesusa had learned about President John Kennedy, as his name was given to several streets in Italia and to a building at their school. When at the University of Heidelberg, they had traveled to Berlin and saw a video of Kennedy's trip to that city in June, 1963. Given their interest in John Kennedy, Dallas was added to their itinerary, before going to New York and then to Notre Dame Cathedral in Paris and then home. Traveling to Dallas was not the preference of the Co-Popes' security team.

In Dallas on Tuesday, January 3, 2045, the trip into the city started well, just as it did for the Kennedy's in 1963. Fifteen minutes later, reality loomed in the form of a drone that was flying toward the popemobile while on the way to the Dallas Book Depository and Dealey Plaza. "What's that?" said more than one visitor to the city who heard or saw the drone. A policeman called in a "red alert" message that a drone was flying toward the papal route. No one knew whether it was armed or whether it was a journalist's effort at getting a better look at the motorcade, but the Dallas Police treated the "alert" as seriously as they could – in the twelve seconds they had left before its possible intersection with the papal route.

Taking a slightly different route than the 1963 Kennedy motorcade, the Co-Popes traveled west on Elm Street and came into Deavey Plaza where Kennedy was shot. Coming from the north, and just after passing through the intersection with Houston Street, the drone fired six 9 mm caliber shots into the popemobile before crashing into it a 130 km/hour. Hitting the windshield, the drone further injured the driver, who had already been hit by two of the bullets, and the car burst into flame. Three other bullets hit the bulletproof glass protector between the driver and the Co-Popes.

The sixth bullet went through the front seat and hit Jesusa's left hand as she was ducking behind that seat. "Oh, my God!" she screamed. The popemobile crashed into a building on Elm Street whereupon police and EMTs descended upon the vehicle and removed Jesus and Jesusa and drove them to the new Parkland Hospital. It was built in 2015, replacing the hospital where John Kennedy was taken and died.

The wound to Jesusa's hand was serious, in the sense that any bullet traveling through a human body is serious, but not life-threatening. There were no broken or shattered bones and no nerves were severed. The radial artery was cut, and it was repaired after the loss of half a liter of her blood. She stayed in the hospital for a day and then she and Jesus continued their tour to New York City, where they addressed the United Nations.

As with others who had survived assassination attempts, such as Theodore and Franklin Roosevelt and Ronald Reagan, the stature of Co-Popes Jesus and Jesusa was enhanced by the near-miss in Dallas. It was even noted that Jesusa's wound was likely in the same location as the nail in the left hand of Jesus of Nazareth.

Jesusa spoke first, and began by saying, "Let us be thankful that the Great Transformation has, so far, brought us back from the brink of nuclear and environmental disaster. However, we have much to do to improve the status of humanity. We must continue to encourage humanity's best traits and discourage our worst. There is goodness in all of us. We know from our history that we, men and women alike, have within us the emotions of hate and murder. We know that those emotions can be stirred up by demagogues, whether they are government officials or media celebrities. Our challenge is dampen those dangerous emotions and to foster the good emotions within us, such as love, happiness, curiosity and hope.

We can improve the behavior of humanity by positively reinforcing good behavior or non-violent behavior and negatively reinforcing bad behavior. This may sound like it came from the 20th century utopian classic, *Walden Two*, because it does. If we know that exposing people, especially young people, to violence in the media causes them to be more violent, then we should take reasonable steps toward reducing that exposure. The primary lesson of that book about the behavioral transformation of people's behavior should not be cast away because of its elitist, anti-democratic flavor. Instead, let's replace the Walden's leader, T.E. Frazier, with democratically elected representatives.

Reinforcing good behavior could involve the teaching of Emotional Education, where students learn about emotions and how to present those emotions to others in positive, constructive ways. It could involve teaching the techniques of mediation and negotiation and support of Peace academies in every nation. Prizes and medals should be given to those who peacefully resolve conflicts, instead of, or in addition to, bestowing awards on military people who kill other people.

To discourage violent behavior, movies, television programs, video games and other media should be assessed a tax roughly equivalent to the external costs of the excess or gratuitous violence as can be fairly allocated. As such an amount is extremely difficult to calculate, a fair estimate would be to double the cost factor where realistic violence exceeds normal frequency in real life, and to triple or quadruple the cost where the violence is unrealistic and excessive. As is sometimes said, the devil is in the details, but some means must be found to discourage such media violence.

The names of the people and corporations who produce such depictions of violence should be exposed for all to see. Just as Transparency International (www.transparency.org) has, for 50 years, beginning in 1995, been publishing its Global Corruption Index, the supporters of non-violence should publish an annual list of the purveyors of violence. Consumers should be encouraged to boycott, or otherwise stigmatize, those purveyors.

Violence in sports can more easily be discouraged, by simply changing the rules. The "no-brainer" place to start, and please pardon the play on words, is to stop the practice of allowing football (formerly called "soccer" in the U.S.) players to "head" the ball. It would also be a "no-brainer" to ban blows to the head in boxing, but that problem can be eliminated by entirely prohibiting boxing, with or without gloves. All related extreme sports and martial arts should no longer be taught to children or tolerated. In brief, any so-called sport which involves the infliction of pain or injury to another person should be banned. On the other hand, wrestling and judo and related sports are tests of skill and strength, and don't involve the intentional infliction of pain; and they can be allowed to continue.

From my days as a student in Boston, and in support of the positive reinforcement of B.F. Skinner and *Walden Two*, I give you now the lyrics of a great songwriter and singer, Johnny Mercer, who wrote and sang the song, "Accentuate the Positive." Now I sing my favorite lyrics:

> You've got to accentuate the positive
> Eliminate the negative
> And latch on to the affirmative
> Don't mess with Mister In-Between
>
> You've got to spread joy up to the maximum
> Bring gloom down to the minimum
> Have faith or pandemonium's
> Liable to walk upon the scene

Let us move forward in that spirit, with song and with a sense of humor. Bless you."

Jesus spoke next, beginning with his recent shock that someone or some group appeared to try to kill him and his sister.

He said, "We had received threats before, but this was the first time that shots had been fired at us. It was a reminder that we still have a long way to go to tame humanity's worst instincts, and correct the damage we have done to the Earth.

Supporting my sister's comments, I emphasize that we support the humanist approach of rewarding behavior that all humans are already programmed to show – unless detoured by behavioral messages of violence. Non-violence is not a complex message. Some of humanity's greatest leaders have advocated and practiced non-violence, including Jesus of Nazareth, Mahatma Gandhi and Martin Luther King, Jr. Please note that it doesn't take great education or intelligence to understand non-violence and the need to present our humane virtues. One of the many American victims of police brutality, Rodney King (no relation to Martin L. King, Jr.) famously said during the 1992 Los Angeles riots that followed the acquittals of his assailants, "Can we all get along?"[4] This is not a complex message.

We are not advocating massive transhumanist changes to the human genetic code. While there have been promising scientific advances in showing how electrical impulses and ingested chemicals can alter human behavior, we are not yet at the point where such technology is available to everyone.

---

4. King's was often misquoted as saying, "Can't we all just get along," but the meaning is nearly the same as the correct version. See the Wikipedia entry at
http://en.wikipedia.org/wiki/Rodney_King

I don't have the musical ear of my sister, but we do share a dream for humanity. That dream was well-stated by Martin Luther King, Jr. in Washington, D.C. in 1963, and I wish to borrow his cadence with my paraphrasing, to say:

> I have a dream that one day the
> sons and daughters of former
> antagonists will be able to sit down
> together at the table of
> brotherhood.
>
> I have a dream that one day even
> our least democratic countries,
> previously sweltering with the heat
> of injustice, and sweltering with
> the heat of oppression, will be
> transformed into oases of freedom
> and justice.
>
> I have a dream that all of our
> children will one day live in a world
> where they will not be judged by
> the color of their skin but by the
> content of their character.
>
> I have a dream today!

We have other dreams, too. That our planet will recover from the damage our forebears have caused and we will again live in harmony and equilibrium with our Earth. Bless you all."

The next day Jesus and Jesusa visited the World Trade Center site, the September 11 museum, and the apartment lobby where John Lennon was murdered. Jesus spoke to the group of reporters of the dangers the world faces if we allow the feelings of hate within all of us to overcome the feelings of love. He said, "I'm sorry to say that religion and religions played a role in that situation by encouraging people to believe that their way was the only way and that those who chose other ways were apostates and enemies. We are now moving away from such dangerous thoughts, but they are still present – as we saw last week in Dallas."

That afternoon, the Dallas police contacted the Popes' entourage to advise that they had arrested a suspect in the attempted murder of Jesus and Jesusa in Dallas. His name was Patrick O'Laughlin and the apparent motive arose from his opposition to the changes in the church since he was a child. When Jesus heard about the call and the arrest, he pulled aside his aide, Father Turkson, and said, "Please contact the Dallas Police Dept. and request that a videocall be arranged among me, Jesusa and O'Laughlin for later in the evening. Let's say, nine o'clock. We'd like to talk with Mr. O'Laughlin."

"But, your Holiness, this is a highly unusual request," said his Ghanian aide, who continued, "I understand that Americans try to keep victims away from accused perpetrators until after the trials."

"Thank you, Father Turkson, but I'm somewhat familiar with the American justice system," replied Jesus. "It's come a long way since they executed innocent people, including Derek Barnabei, the American of Italian heritage, in 2000. However, they have more to do before the U.S. justice system is as good as its lawyers claim. Let's take an active role in this case, even if the lawyers, prosecutors and police don't recommend it."

After dinner, the connection was made. O'Laughlin was in Dallas with his attorney, Craig Watkins, Jr.

"How do you do, Mr. O'Laughlin," began Jesusa. "I'm Pope Jesusa and this is Pope Jesus, but please address us by our familiar names, Jesus and Jesusa."

"How do you do, your holinesses. Sorry, that's what I was advised to call you," replied O'Laughlin.

Jesus reassured him, "That's OK. Please address us as Jesus and Jesusa and we will call you Patrick."

Jesusa stepped in, "Look, Patrick. We have heard of assassination attempts in the U.S., and one of our predecessors, Pope Ionnes Paulus II was shot and nearly killed in 1981 in Roma. He forgave his assailant, Mehmet Ali Agca, who was released after 19 years. Do you think we should forgive you?"

O'Laughlin had been eager to speak, "I do, but I don't. You see, I had nothing to do with the firing of those shots at you. I was flying that drone, but I had no intention of hurting you, let alone killing you. I'm innocent. Why should I ask for forgiveness for something I didn't do?"

"That's a good question," Jesus said.

Attorney Watkins added, "I understand that you have been interested in wrongful convictions, and I hope that this case doesn't become one like the Barnabei case. It seems to have that potential, however."

"Ok," said Jesusa. "We just assumed that we would be talking with someone who might be willing to talk with us about what he did. However, it appears that, once again, assumption can be a problem. It looks like we cannot help you right now, beyond wishing you good luck in your efforts to achieve justice; but let us know if you need help."

"Wait," said Patrick. "It's true that I dislike some of the changes in the church. In fact, I don't think that we should have a woman pope or co-pope, or whatever. No offense to you personally, Jesusa, of course, but it's wrong. It's not how I was brought up."

"Well, I can understand, Patrick," said Jesusa. "It wasn't how I was brought up, either. That is, I never expected to see a woman pope, or even a co-pope, but that doesn't mean that when the opportunity arose I should have refused it."

"Nope, I suppose not," said Patrick. "Another thing. Why do you talk with Muslims? They're terrorists."

Responded Jesus, "Only a few people in any society are hardwired true criminals. There was a time, earlier in this century, and before, that some Muslims saw violence as the only way to show their frustrations with the high Muslim unemployment and Western secular or Christian wealth. We think the better answer to unemployment is birth control for men and women who want it. Well, that's a bit oversimplified, but a high birth rate, coupled with dramatic reductions in death rates, was a reason for the large proportion of young Muslims, and hence, their unemployment. With so many young people, there were not enough wise elders around to counsel them toward peaceful solutions. Back to your question. We think it's important to talk with everybody who wishes to talk with you, especially with those of different views. Hence our call to you this evening."

Jesusa looked at the clock on the ceiling, "Patrick, it's getting late here in New York. We have to go, as we leave tomorrow morning. Good luck to you. If the system works and you are telling us the truth, you should be found innocent. In fact, your case shouldn't even go to trial, but bigger mistakes have been made. Thanks goodness the death penalty has been abolished. Keep in touch. Let us know if we can help. If you have any idea of how your drone happened to shoot at us and almost kill us, please tell the police. We have to go."

"Ok. Thanks. Bye. Ciao," said Patrick.

The next day, they flew to London to meet with the Archbishop of Canterbury, Thomasina More, who had been the church's leader since 2034, the 500th anniversary of its separation from the Catholic Church. Before their world tour began in May, the Co-Popes had begun negotiations with the Anglican Church, together with its U.S. partner, the Episcopal Church. By the time they arrived in London, it was clear that negotiations were proceeding satisfactorily and that a reunification of the churches was probable in 2046. Jesus and Jesusa then met with King William V and then left for Paris and finally Roma.

The assassination attempt in Dallas caused worldwide revulsion at the widespread availability of guns and weapons in the United States, and spurred that country finally to enact more stringent rules for guns, including an amendment to the U.S. Constitution which provided that the States and the Federal Government "could regulate the manufacture, sale and possession of firearms and ammunition as was necessary to promote the general welfare."

Chapter 8 2045 to Resignation

Upon their return to Roma just before Christmas, 2045, the Co-Popes sought renewal and growth within the Church. They recognized that some conservative Catholics had left the church because, as they said, "The Church has left us." However, the way forward was to recruit people who sought a little more than the pure rationality of the IHEU, from which they had resigned as co-presidents. They could have continued as co-presidents of both organizations, but they realized that they needed to focus on one, and the spiritual attraction of the Roman Catholic Church led to their choice.

It was similar to the choice Robert E. Lee made when the southern states formed the Confederacy and seceded from the northern states. As a loyal solider of the United States Army for 32 years, since 1829, it was a wrenching decision to transfer his loyalty to the State of Virginia and the Confederacy. He did this, even after being offered by President Lincoln the command of the entire U.S. Army. Sometimes, two masters cannot be served.

Jesus and Jesusa were familiar with Lee's decision, from their studies in Boston, but they sought not to suffer the disastrous consequences which befell him. The Catholic Church was now a smaller organization than the IHUE, but it had a rich history and a profound responsibility to bring its members into the 21st century.

There had been many reforms, and many details needed to be resolved.

Over the next 20 years, the Church finally pulled itself away from the moral and financial disasters of child abuse which had been brought on by the now-abandoned policies of celibacy for priests, and prohibitions against women and homosexual priests. It was estimated by a special commission that fully one-third of the entire wealth of the Catholic Church, including its art and real estate, was consumed by compensation to the people injured by those earlier policies. Much property had to be sold, and much was given to governments and non-profit organizations as the Church could no longer afford to maintain them.

In April, 2046, Jesus and Jesus were advised by email[1] from Attorney Watkins that Patrick O'Laughlin was convicted of two counts of attempted murder and was sentenced to life in prison. Watkins apologized for not asking them to help during the trial, by submitting a video victim statement. He said he thought that the trial was going so well that he felt that he didn't need their help. The prosecution didn't need them as witnesses, as the entire event of January 3 was recorded on several video devices.

Jesus asked Jesusa, "What should we do? I know I can be naive about people and gullible too, but O'Laughlin didn't seem so angry that he would have tried to kill us. I believed him when we talked by videophone."

Jesusa agreed. "Let's ask Mother Scheck, the lawyer priest who helped set up the original interview among you, me and Patrick O'Laughlin, to look into the case and see if she can help. Perhaps she can conclusively find that he really did send the drone to kill us, or she can help exonerate him. She's a tough person. She went to the University of Texas Law School when she was a nun. Just after she became an attorney, the Vaticano Council III decreed in 2023 that women could become priests. One unanticipated consequence of that decision was that the role of nuns was thrown into uncertainty. As Sister Teresa Scheck, she had done considerable research on how American male-only colleges had become co-educational and the

1. jesusandjesusa@vaticano.org. [As of 2014, not a real email address.]

effects of those changes on the diminishing number of women's colleges. Similarly, the equalization of women in the U.S. military led to the dismantling of women-only units. Sister Scheck proposed in 2028 the very simple solution that all nuns be automatically ordained as priests except for those who wished to continue their careers or lives as nuns.

Similarly, monks had always been able to work as priests, or they could elect to be solely members of monasteries. In 2030, there were 555,000 Roman Catholic nuns and 108,000 monks, worldwide. Both populations were significantly less than 100 years earlier. In 2030, Pope Francesco II issued a papal "bull" that adopted Sister Scheck's proposal, which had been endorsed by all the major orders of nuns. Henceforth, she was known as "Mother Scheck." The previous title for the managing nuns of convents, "Mother Superior," was changed to "Bishop."

Jesus and Jesusa talked with Mother Scheck and she agreed to work on the O'Laughlin case full-time for the next six months.

In 2047, the one-month global religious conclave was held in Arusha, Tanzania, as was planned in the 2045 Temple Mount Accord. Arusha is about three hours from Mount Kilimanjaro, which became an international symbol of global warming when it lost its last snowpack in 2023. Attending the conclave were leaders from the major religions of the world, together with the IHUE and other humanist organizations. Giving the welcoming address was Pope Emeritus Francesco II, who lived in the nearby Franciscan monastery.

At its conclusion, the draft "Kilimanjaro Accord" was issued and distributed to the members of participating organizations and through the media to everyone in the world. The draft agreement combined the Temple Mount Accord of 2045 with the IHUE's 2018 Geneva Declaration. Paragraphs were added to emphasize the need for mutual education about other faiths and mutual tolerance. A protocol was established for a World Values Forum (WVF) which would meet semi-annually to discuss how the world's faiths can reach common moral and ethical ground on specific issues, such as marriage and death. The WVF was intentionally designed to parallel the older and richly endowed World Economic Forum which began in 1971 in Davos, Switzerland.

The Kilimanjaro Accord was ratified by all the major religions of the world, and by the IHUE. The signing ceremony was scheduled for December 10, 2048, the 100th anniversary of the adoption by the United Nations of the Universal Declaration of Human Rights. Article 18 of that Declaration, was especially applicable. It reads:

Everyone has the right to freedom of thought, conscience and religion; this right includes freedom to change his religion or belief, and freedom, either alone or in community with others and in public or private, to manifest his religion or belief in teaching, practice, worship and observance.

One of the intended effects of the reconciliation among religions was the nearly complete elimination of religion-based violent acts. No longer were the clergy of any religion calling for any harm to be caused to any member of any other religion. The common ground was mutual tolerance.

During the reign of Co-Popes Jesus and Jesusa, the Catholic Church supported the "Great Transformation" until its formal pre-determined end in 2070. In its place, the "Great Transformation II," also scheduled for 50 years, was proposed by the United Nations Secretary-General Malia Obama and later ratified by the General Assembly. Obama had been

Secretary-General since 2045, and this was her last major project. She had long since exceeded her original goal of serving the U.N. for longer than her heroine, Eleanor Roosevelt, who served nine years from 1946 until 1953 and again from 1961-62, and was substantially responsible for the U.N. passage of the Universal Declaration of Human Rights in 1948. The Catholic Church, as the Holy See, rather than in its former status as the city-state, Vaticano, was a co-sponsor of the Universal Declaration.

The "Great Transformation II" sought by the end of 2120 these goals:

1. Through the continued reduction of the greenhouse gasses, the reversal of global warming. One flake of sought-after evidence of that reversal would be the return of a snow pack, year-round, to Mt. Kilimanjaro, perhaps before the death of Pope Emeritus Francesco II.

2. The continued reduction of the human population to 6 billion, which was the level last seen in 1999. Further reductions in the population should continue until approximately reaching one billion, which was the population around 1800. The United Nations Demography Office predicted and advocated for the following milestones in global population:

2100	6 billion
2125	5
2150	4
2180	3
2220	2
2300	1

    Alternatively, a team of scientists was to be assembled to determine the level of human population whereby humanity can exist in equilibrium with other species on the Earth. It's been predicted that such a number would be between the 1800 population of one billion and the 1925 population of two billion.

3. The continued reduction in the incarceration of people, through the reduction of crime, especially violent crime, and the use of alternate methods of punishment.

Back in Texas, Attorney Scheck read all she could from the online records of the O'Laughlin case. Then she contacted the "Free Patrick Committee" which was led by Patrick's former roommate, Arnie Benedict.

She asked him, "Arnie, or do you prefer to be called Arnold? Why does the committee want to see Patrick freed?"

" 'Arnie' is good," he answered. "We think Patrick should be freed because he didn't mean to have the drone actually fire a weapon."

"How do you know that?" asked Scheck.

"Well, I just know. As Patrick testified at his trial, he was just trying to scare the City of Dallas and Texas, and even the United States, into doing something about gun control. Weirdly, he didn't like having Co-Popes, either, so scaring them seemed okay, too. He had created his drone for hunting feral pigs, which is why it had an infrared sensor on it. But he didn't want to kill the popes."

Then Arnie introduced Scheck to his wofriend, Jane Joplin. Mother Scheck thought it curious that Joplin was Patrick's wofriend before the attack on the popes and the trial. Also, Arnie told her that he, too, was skilled with building and flying drones and that he and Patrick had worked together on the drone involved in the attack on the popes. Arnie was not asked to testify at Patrick's trial.

Mother Scheck then traveled to the Coffield State Prison in Tennessee Colony, near Dallas to visit Patrick O'Laughlin. After introductions, she asked him, "Why did you send that drone toward Co-Popes Jesus and Jesusa?"

"Well," began Patrick, "I didn't like the Co-Popes, and don't think they should have been popes, especially the woman. But I didn't plan to hurt them. My plan was to scare them, and maybe then they would resign."

"Did you really think they might resign?" asked Scheck.

"Well, not really. But my other idea was that I was getting sick of too many people having drones and not knowing what they were doing. There have been several crashes recently. We ought to be certified and licensed. I know it sounds funny, because I had drones, but I knew what I was doing, and I needed drones for my work of finding and killing feral pigs for farmers in Texas. Those pigs were ruining lots of cash crops."

"So what's the connection?" asked Scheck.

"Well, I figured that if a drone got close to the Co-Popes, Texas might take seriously the need to regulate them, before somebody got hurt."

"Interesting. Did you explain that to your jury?" asked Scheck.

"Well, I started to, but the damn prosecutor cut me off and said what I was saying was irrelevant, irrelevant, or whatever," said Patrick. He continued, "Then a juror asked a question about what I said by sending a note to the judge, but the judge told the court that he would not allow the question. She said that my political views were not on trial, just my conduct. I think she misunderstood the question. In any case, my lawyer then blew it off, and questioned me about something else."

Attorney Scheck wished that she had been Patrick's attorney at the time, because she would have argued to have Patrick continue that part of his testimony. She asked Patrick, "If you didn't intend to kill the Co-Popes or even hurt them, why do you think the drone fired at them."

Patrick responded, "That's a good question. You might even call it the 64,000 mundo question. I don't know. I didn't push the trigger. At least I didn't think I did, and I had no intention to do that. But when the guns were fired, I panicked and pressed the "crash" button, which shut off the engines and inadvertently sent the drone into the popemobile."

"But you don't know?" asked Scheck, stumped.

"Funny thing was, Arnie and I had talked about installing an automatic firing mechanism, based on the heat of the pigs, but I said it wasn't a good idea, and I wouldn't add such a mechanism to our drone."

"Could Arnie have installed it without your knowing?" asked the priest attorney.

"Well, I asked him that question at some point after the trial, and he said he didn't," said Arnie, with less confidence. "Before the trial, I thought of it, but I assumed that Arnie would have told me, because we were close friends. Then I saw after my trial that Jane didn't move out of our suite with Arnie. She stayed there and hooked up with him. Made me wonder a little."

"What would such a switch look like and what parts would it have had?

"It would be a switch connected to the wires from the pyroelectric crystals of the infared sensor to the videocam. The switch would have a voltage sensor which would be triggered when the infared signals increased, like when the drone got close to the pigs. Come to think of it, that sensor wouldn't have to have gotten as close to the popemobile, because its engine was hot."

"Ok, thanks," said Attorney Scheck. "I'll check with the police and have a look at the remains of the drone in the evidence room."

Mother Scheck then went to the Dallas Police Dept. and met with Lieutenant Friday who was the officer who testified at Patrick's trial about the drone and its capabilities.

Attorney Scheck asked Lt. Josephine Friday, "Were there any parts that you didn't understand or were able to identify?"

"I don't think so, but let's go take another look."

In the evidence room, they spread the pieces out on the table.

"What's in that clear red bag?" asked Scheck.

"Right! I forgot about that," said Lt. Friday. She then said, "There was a voltage sensor with wires to nowhere, which we couldn't figure out."

"Would the wires have been long enough to reach the electronic trigger mechanism of the gun?" asked Attorney Scheck.

"Don't know. Let me check," answered Friday. "First, let's look at the schematic I drew of the reconstructed drone. Okay. Here's the electric trigger and here's the infared sensor. Yup. The wires were long enough."

Then, both women looked carefully at the area around the electronic trigger and found two tiny soldering points, one for each wire.

"Looks like the voltage sensor could have triggered the firing and the voltage sensor responded to the strength of the infared sensor. Never seen anything like this," said Lt. Friday.

"Me neither, of course," said Attorney Scheck. "I'm going to go back to ask Arnie Benedict a few more questions. You could come, but I think it would be better if I went alone. I'll even wear my clerical collar."

Mother Scheck called Arnie and arranged a followup meeting at a local coffee shop that he chose.

Scheck began, "As I mentioned on the phone, I've learned more about the drone since I talked with you yesterday. What can you tell me about an automatic trigger in the drone?"

Arnie struggled to respond. "Okay. You know. I thought we could get through this and get Patrick out of prison without my having to admit what I did. I didn't mean to hurt anyone. I just installed the automatic trigger to show Patrick how it would work with feral pigs. I didn't know that he was going to fly the drone toward the Co-Popes when they came to Dallas. More importantly, I forgot to de-activate the automatic trigger after I installed it. I thought Patrick was going to hunt feral pigs that night, but he didn't. Instead, the next day, he flew it toward the Co-Popes. I guess I'm in trouble now, right?"

Relieved the exoneration of Patrick was in sight, Scheck was sincerely concerned about Arnie's plight and said, "You need to retain an attorney, and he or she should help you to do what's right for you and for Patrick. He should not be in prison. And another thing. What Jane decides to do is important, too. Right now, it looks like you set up Patrick in order to get his wofriend."

"No, that wasn't it at all," responded Arnie. "It's true that I was attracted to her, but my leaving the electronic trigger activated was an accident. I'll be happy to take a polygraph or a polyvoicegraph test. Jane agonized about our relationship, and she went to Patrick to ask for his permission and he said it was okay for her to be with me. He said to her, 'It looks like I'm here for life, despite Arnie's efforts to get me out of here, but you have to move on with your life. If you love Arnie, go for it.' "

With the support of his new attorney, Arnie later took both tests and passed both of them. His attorney contacted the Dallas Prosecutor's Conviction Integrity

Unit and there was a meeting, together with Patrick's lawyer, to discuss the options.

The result was a plea bargain for Patrick to plead guilty to criminal assault for intending to fly his drone close enough to the Co-Popes to scare them. His prison sentence was reduced to time served. Like many people wrongly convicted of crimes they did not commit, Patrick did something wrong, but just not as wrong as the crime for which he was convicted. Unfortunately, by pleading guilty to a felony, he waived any right for compensation for the wrongly convicted. Arnie plead guilty to reckless endangerment and was sentenced to two years of community service.

Upon hearing the news, Jesus and Jesusa called Patrick and Arnie separately and forgave them both.

Said Jesus, "We invite you both to come to Roma at a time of your choosing." They agreed on a visit in two weeks, during which time they would sit down for at least one frank discussion.

In 2071 the Co-Popes traveled to England to celebrate the 25th anniversary of the 2046 reunification of the Roman Catholic and the Anglican Church, together with the U.S. Episcopalian partner. Greeting Jesus and Jesusa at Buckingham Palace was 30-year old Queen Georgiana, who had become queen the previous year upon the abdication of her father, King George VII. Georgiana sought some private spiritual guidance with Jesusa. They went to a private place and the queen asked, "What do you think about inherited titles? Does the practice seem right to you?"

Jesusa answered, "It's an interesting question, as the unusual circumstances of Jesus's and my births was said to have influenced our subsequent election as Co-Popes. It could have been argued that we inherited our positions. In our travels, we have met several monarchs who have indicated their discomfort with their inherited status. A few years after our 2045 world tour visit to Thailand, the queen there abdicated, but made her abdication conditional upon the abolition by the Thai parliament of the monarchy. What do you think?"

Georgiana thought for a moment and then answered, "Inherited status doesn't seem right to me, and being selected at birth for a position in the government, even if not as large a role as it used to be, seems unfair. The status we inherit should be equal to everyone else. Also, this really isn't the kind of work I want to do. I could abdicate, but that would just leave the problem for someone else to resolve. If you look at the course of history, it's easy to see where the future of monarchy is going – nowhere."

Jesusa responded, "It sounds like you know what you should do. Here's the private phone number of the former Thai queen, Suvahana. Maybe you would want to call her. Good luck. We should now rejoin the others."

Jesus and Jesusa, and Queen Georgiana participated in the 25th anniversary service at Canterbury Cathedral, which was conducted by Archbishop Chad Mercia.

Over the next few years, Pope Jesusa and Queen Georgiana talked by phone about the issue of a monarchy and in April, 2076, Queen Georgiana told Jesusa of her plan, which was very similar to that executed by Thai Queen Suvahana in 2048. Later that year, she had several discussions of her plan with her family, including her father, the former King George VII, who disagreed strongly with the plan, and with Prime Minister Diana Thatcher. Queen Georgiana scheduled an address to the nation for July 4, 2076.

She said to the people of the United Kingdom, "It is time to recognize the truth of what the American colonists told us 300 years ago in 1776, that all people are created equal, and there can be no exception for a few families blessed to inherit titles and countries. Therefore, I am today announcing my plan to abdicate as Queen next April 23, 2077, St. George's Day, conditional upon the enactment of legislation by the Parliament to abolish the monarchy and our system of nobility. Over the next several months, I am confident that Prime Minister Thatcher's government and I will work out a reasonable path forward on these matters."

Jesus and Jesusa were impressed by Queen Georgiana's determination which led to the end of the British monarchy in 2077. She and her husband, still in their 30s, went to work for the World Wildlife Fund.

The Co-Popes continued their reigns but at a slower pace. The major reforms were over, but the continued decline in the numbers of priests and, more importantly, members or congregants in the Catholic Church, forced the Co-Popes to be in forever downsizing mode. It was not a happy process. They were in reasonable health, but it was time for a new generation of leaders for the Church.

Finally, in May, 2083 they announced that they would resign the next year on May 30, 2084, which would be their 70th birthday. At that time, their 40 year reigns would be the longest in Church history. Until the Pope Benedictus XVI resignation in 2013, there had not been a papal resignation since Pope Gregorius XII in 1415. That resignation came after he convened the Council of Constance which ended the Avignon Exile. Thus, in the last 500 years, there had been only three resignations before those of Jesus and Jesusa, with all of them in the 21st century: Pope Benedictus XVI in 2013, Pope Francesco I in 2026, and Pope Francesco II in 2044.

At the recommendation of Co-Popes Jesus and Jesusa, the College of Cardinals elected Cardinal Susanna Bakhita of Sudan as Pope. She earned the respect of Pope Francesco II and her peer cardinals with her successful efforts to bring equality for women in Africa and the complete ability and right to control their reproduction. This work included reaching

consensus with the Muslims to whom she brought the
message from the Qur'an that Islam supports families,
and that the best families come when parents want
children and less to when they arrive by accident. She
cited the statement from the Qur'an, "You should not
kill your children for fear of want"[2] and interpreted
that as meaning that good Muslims prevented children
from being conceived where they could not be properly
fed, educated and loved. This approach was most
effective with poor Muslims. Rich Muslims needed no
religious affirmation, as they were already having
smaller, less than replacement size, families for other
reasons. Most importantly, Cardinal Bakhita did not
preach this message directly to Muslims. Instead she
met with women of all faiths and together they
developed consensus that was said to arise from all
the religions of Africa. Afterwards, the messages were
communicated by social networks and other people-to-
people media.

Pope Bakhita became the first unitary woman pope
and the first from Africa.

2. Qur'an (17:31, 6:151)

Chapter 9 Aging and Death

Jesus and Jesusa retired as popes emerita to their childhood home in Salerno. Their parents, Giuseppe and Maria, had died a few years earlier and the twins inherited their home. Giuseppe died of pneumonia in 2076 at the age of 97. Called "the poor man's friend" because it delivers a dignified painless death to its sufferers, pneumonia came at the time that Giuseppe was becoming bedridden due to arthritis and related joint and bone ailments. Always an active man, Giuseppe had long agreed with Maria that he did not want to live as a burden to others, and especially to his wife.

Maria continued for three more years, with failing health. She had stated to her children that she wanted to live to be 100, but that was enough. Three months after her 100th birthday in 2078, Maria died with the assistance of her doctor and a humane dosage of drugs. She drank the medicines and said to Jesus and Jesusa, "Good-bye and thank you. You have made me very proud. I love you both."

After their mother's death, Jesus and Jesus kept the family home and used it for occasional vacations, until their retirement in 2084. It was modest, but more comfortable for them than the vast papal retreat at Castel Gandolfo, to which Pope Benedictus XVI had retired. Pope Francesco I had returned to Argentina to his former home, and Pope Francesco II retired to Tanzania.

Although their energy was diminished, they still tried to respond to the requests for help from inmates claiming wrongful conviction. The letters from Italian inmates were referred to the Italia Innocence Project at the Universita degli Studi di Milano, and the others were referred to the Global Innocence Network (GIN) which was headquartered in New York. Fortunately, the numbers of such requests were declining as the estimated percentage of wrongful convictions was close to the Great Transformation Organization goal of .1%.

As was the experience of other cloned mammals, the bodies of Jesus and Jesusa declined faster than others, after the age of approximately 65. Earlier in their lives, they made a pact to leave this world together, just as they had come into the world together. If they had a choice, and were not otherwise taken by accident or paralyzing disease or assassination, they would commit suicide together. In March, 2089, Jesus had a stroke, causing a fall in the garden and he was partially paralyzed. In April, Jesusa was diagnosed with a new form of dementia, i.e. one that defied the previously developed cures for Alzheimer's disease and other related illnesses.

They knew their time to die was coming, and it did not scare them. They decided to take their lives on their 75th birthday, on May 30, 2089, in the presence of their closest friends. Jesusa would quote one of her heroines, Charlotte Perkins Gilman, who wrote in her own suicide note 154 years earlier, "It is the simplest of human rights to choose a quick and easy death in place of a slow and horrible one."

Instead of using a helium "exit bag" which imposed some obligation on those accompanying suicides during their last moments, Jesus and Jesusa chose to drink a suicide medicine in their bedroom. With the help of a doctor, and the previous successful experiences of millions around the world, they chose red wine with codeine, pentobartitol, and seconal.

They toasted each other and their friends, and then "to the eternal survival and goodness of humanity." Pursuant to the requests of Jesus and Jesusa in their wills, their bodies were cremated at the solar crematorium in Salerno and their ashes were combined. The co-mingled ashes were then taken to the Vaticano and entombed in the Sacristry together with most of their predecessor popes and not far from the "Holy Prepuce," formerly of Calcata.

Chapter 10 Post Script

Elvira Sediva, attorney, and the executor of the estate of Alessandro Galvani, had heard the rumors that Jesus and Jesusa would commit suicide at some symbolic time. Working as an attorney in Salerno, Elvira knew much about the twins, but her interest in the retired co-popes became more focused in 2076 upon the death of her client, Alessandro Galvani.

Galvani had created a "Last Testament" as part of his will and it was to be communicated to the executors of the estates of Jesus and Jesusa upon their deaths, and later to the public. Galvani's last statement read as follows:

> In 2013, I was a member of the team of five scientists, headed by Professor Angelo Pappalardo, which created the two cloned embryos which were implanted into the womb of Maria Prescelto of Salerno in August of that year. Her two children, Jesus and Jesusa Prescelto, were born on May 30, 2014.
>
> As a member of the team, I was devoted to its success. We were competing with other universities for prominence and for grants from international foundations.
>
> The team extracted DNA from the "Holy Prepuce" and my fellow team members were optimistic that the DNA could be successfully altered to produce a male and female being after being inserted into two donor ova. However, I was very confident that the procedure would fail. Therefore, at a critical time, I substituted my own stem cells to the

project before the gender differentiation stage. Their nuclei were successfully implanted into the two ova, and the nuclei of the donor eggs were removed.

The team was surprised at its success and I was criticized at the time for my pessimism. In fact, I wanted the project to succeed for the institutional reasons mentioned above, but also because I was hopeful that the resulting human beings would be helpful in improving the world. Regarding that latter goal, my hopes were greatly exceeded.

Jesus and Jesusa are excellent co-popes and have done much to save humanity from itself and I didn't want to do or say anything during their lifetimes which would impair their work to move the world to a more reason-based level. When asked, they always tried to deflect questions about their origin, and preferred to restate that they were humans, born of humans. As they chose not to reproduce themselves, there are no children which would be affected by my posthumous revelation of the truth about their origin.

This statement is also about the truth of the science of cloning humans. The truth is that our "Salerno team" did not successfully clone a human using the DNA of a 2,000 year old fragment of skin.

Date: July 6, 2063
Alessandro Galvani /s/

In early June, 2089, a few days after the deaths of Jesus and Jesusa, Attorney Sediva hand-carried

Alessandro Galvani's "Last Testament" to the executors of the estates of Jesus and Jesusa. The executors and Sediva worked on a joint public statement which was released a month later. The release stated,

"It has come to our attention that the circumstances of the births of Jesus and Jesusa were not as they and their parents were told 52 years ago upon their graduation from Universitat Heidelberg. The human cells from which their embryos came were actually from a member of the team of scientists which was working on the cloning project. His name was Alessandro Galvani, and his "Last Testament" is attached to this release. He died in 2069, and by the terms of his will, he mandated that his statement be released only after latter of the deaths of Jesus and Jesusa, without knowing, of course, that they would die on the same day.

All their lives, Jesus and Jesusa distanced themselves from the claims of their origin and, instead, proclaimed themselves humans born of humans, like everyone else.

We believe that this new information changes nothing about the work of Jesus and Jesusa to improve the world and assist in the Great Transformation of the role of humans on Earth from agents of destruction to participants in rebirth and equilibrium."

The sky did not fall when the truth became known around the globe in seconds. Most of the people in the increasingly sophisticated world knew that there was something amiss with the nearly miraculous story. However, belief in the births cloned from the Holy Prepuce did not hamper the work of Jesus and Jesusa, and even contributed to their sense of humor and perspective.

Afterword: The Global Impact of the book, *Jesus and Jesusa*

The novella, *Jesus and Jesusa*, changed the course of world history in ways reminiscent of other books, such as the *Communist Manifesto*, *On the Origin of Species*, *Uncle Tom's Cabin*, and *Silent Spring*.

By reading this novella, which showed what could happen in the world from 2014 onward, the realm of the possible was opened for humanity to see, and it paved the way for progressive change.

For more information, see the summary of the 2093 Ph.D. Thesis of Charlotte Amalie Perkins, The Global Social and Political Impact of the Utopian Novella *Jesus and Jesusa* as presented in Appendix B of the book, *2121*, by Morrison Bonpasse, to be published in 2014. *2121* is a utopian novel about the world through 2121 A.D. as it should be or could be.

www.ingramcontent.com/pod-product-compliance
Lightning Source LLC
Chambersburg PA
CBHW070756120626
46557CB00002B/628